BAD BLOOD
PART II

JANE BRITTAN

BLOWFISH BOOKS

BLOWFISH BOOKS

First published in Great Britain in 2017
by Blowfish Books
Blowfish Books Ltd,
15 Bennerley Road,
London SW11 6DR
www.blowfishbooks.com

ISBN: 978-0-9932334-6-3

Also available as an ebook
Mobi ISBN: 978-0-9932334-7-0
Epub ISBN: 978-0-9932334-8-7

A catalogue record for this book is available
from the British Library.

Typeset by Chandler Book Design

Printed and bound by
Booksfactory Print Group Sp. z o.o. Poland

For my father

Praise for Bad Blood Part One

Four months after his father's suicide, Ben comes home from school to find a mysterious letter telling him to find The Red Gull. This gripping tale constantly builds in suspense until the final shocking twist and an author's after note which made me gasp out loud.

Caroline Ambrose
Bath Children's Novel Award

Twisting, Absorbing, enjoyable

Tony Collins
Author of Open Verdict: 25 Mysterious
Deaths in the Defence Industry

A roller-coaster of a journey through conspiracy theories, hugely believable characters, and some spine-chilling edge-of-cliff climaxes.

Stephen King
School Libraries Association

*Instead of being another copy-cat thriller hanging off the coat tails of the genre's success in the past couple of years, Brittan brings an interesting new twist on this genre which will keep you switched on and unable to put the book down. The fact that **Bad Blood** is in to two parts is the ultimate tease. The need to find out what will happen in Ben's future, if he will reunite with Sophy and if Rees will continue to come after him is strong and I for one can't wait for the release of Part Two.*

Books for Keeps

I read this book in a matter of days and was deeply enthralled by its captivating story line and fascinating characters. Whilst reading it you find yourself trying to solve the mysteries and then being so far from the answers behind the twists, it's mind blowing. I urge you to read Bad Blood, you will not regret it

Amy Steiner
Student

1

There's a taste in my mouth like sour sweat. No matter how much I swallow, it stays there. On my tongue and around my teeth.

The air's heavy like water.

I'm going in circles.

I headed upwards out of the valley towards the ridge like he told me before I left – before he locked the gate and walked away. It took hours, clawing my way through tree roots and scree. Toe by toe, looking for the track we came in on. Once, a helicopter blade clipped the dark canopy above me, scattering a shower of creepers and starting a caterwaul of angry shrieks from the treetops.

I reached the ridge by night fall. Noises from the valley below were carried up in the steaming air: urgent cries, panic, gun shots. I lay back on flat ground and closed my eyes feeling the earth turning under me. I lay there for a few minutes, and when I opened them, it was dark – a dense, breathing dark that hurt my eyes.

I rolled away from the lip of the valley, pitched myself into a shallow dip in the forest floor and slept where I lay.

That was yesterday. The heat wakes me, sharp and close. I shuck off my jacket and push up on my elbows. My skin's blistered with bites, and sweat's pooling at my neck and waist. It's quiet in the valley now, and when I look down, there are thin black plumes of smoke from far below. My father's work – his life. And he's in my head again: his eyes, his fingers hooked through the wire, closing on mine; then the back of him, stiff and square, walking away towards the lab. My father – his valediction: what he wanted, what he did, and the price he paid to undo it all. And the price he made me pay. And what I do with it all when I get home.

The sun's high in the sky before I get going again. I stay high up and head west, looking for the dirt track in the green.

But the undergrowth is so dense, it's all you can do just to shoulder your way through it. It twists and weaves away from you, until, before you know it, you're facing the way you've come. Running's impossible. It's knitted itself together and you can't break it – all you can do is work your way around it. Slowly. Tearing and teasing the whiskery vines: lifting them over my head, while all around me, the forest grubs and calls and scratches.

To move forward at any speed, I have to dip down and so lose the ridge line. Without it, I can't get my bearings. And by dusk on the second day, I'm so lost I can't tell which is up or down. And I need water. I can feel my insides drying, sucking in away from my skin – contracting. Even standing still I can feel my pulse driving. I spend a while trying to lap water from a thin runnel on a leaf but the taste of it makes me gag.

I'm going in circles.

When it gets dark, I know I should spend the night off the ground but I just can't get it together. I lie where I fall again, and close my eyes.

I must have slept because a cramp in my leg wakes me and I'm rubbing and squeezing at my calf when I hear it. The sound of breathing: shallow and chokey. It stops after a minute, and I wait – hold my breath. And I know before I know, that there's someone else out here. Close. Close enough to smell him. Something different. Chemical maybe. Whatever it is, it doesn't belong out here – like me.

I can try and stay hidden or I can make a run for it. Every instinct is telling me to move. Except for I can't see a thing and any movement might just send me hurtling down the valley or cut me in two on a vine.

I listen again, craning my neck in the darkness: nothing. But I know someone's out there.

It's now or never. If I can't see in this, then neither can he, and right now I don't think I'd hesitate to kill anyone who tried to stop me getting home.

Slowly I get onto my knees. Leaf litter whispers under my weight. I reach up blindly for a hold and pull myself up on a branch. I stand up and steady myself. Silence. Then movement: a crack, a shift, and it's unmistakeable – footsteps. I hold my breath. I hold everything. The very exertion of staying still is making me sweat: I can feel it on my eyebrows, my upper lip. My arms are extended, my hands around the branch above me. And then everything is very still, and then it isn't, because whoever it is, crashes in to me from behind and grabs the branch for support. A human hand, hot and wet, clamps over my own, and we fall together onto the forest floor.

I'm shouting, 'Get off me! Get off me!' and I'm thrashing and pumping with my feet and fists, and whoever it is, is pushing me back. I deliver a sharp kick at him but the force of it sends me flying. He's on me at once like a cat. He takes my face in his hands, and pinches tight. His breath is sour and yeasty.

'Stop it! Stop it. It's OK! Stop!'

It's a girl.

I shuffle backwards on my arse and hunch my knees into my chest. She follows. For what seems like forever, we sit there breathing heavily and I'm aware of her rubbing her sides.

She winces.

I say gruffly, 'I'm sorry. I'm sorry I hit you. I didn't know –'

The blackness presses in on us.

She shifts her weight, whispers, 'I am OK.'

'Yeah. Well. I'm sorry anyway. I don't hit girls.'

Is she laughing? I can't tell.

She gets a little closer. 'Where are you from?'

'England. I'm English. Why?'

'English. Ah. English men are always sorry.'

'Well I am. Who are you?'

She whispers, 'My name is Yun.'

'How come you speak English?'

'Because I learned it. What's your name?'

'Ben.'

'Ben. Ben. Ben,' she laughs a little.

'What's so funny?

'Is sound like Peng. Chinese boy name. It means … bird … big bird.'

Her laugh is like a child's. Like music.

'Right. Yun … do you know the way to the road?'

'What road?'

'The … you know … the track? To get down?'

'To get down?'

'To get away from the valley.' And I realise I'm pointing like an idiot when we can't even see each other's faces. She's quiet for a long time then. I hear the soft rustle of her shirt as she breathes.

'You come from laogai?' she says.

I hesitate and then I say, 'The camp? Yes. Yes. The laogai. I was there for a long time.'

'But you're not Chinese?'

'No.'

'So why you –?'

'I –'

'Are you a bad man?'

'What? Look, no. I'm –'

'You escaped …' she says.

'Yes,' and he's in my head again, bumping against the sides. It hurts too much to think about him. I think perhaps the only way I'm going to get out of here is to pretend like he never existed – like he was never there.

'The camp is broken,' she says.

'Yes.'

'Something very bad happening there – very … making poison, making –'

'You heard that? Where did you hear that?'

'Everybody knows it. People very scared.'

For a minute, I sit and rock back and forward with my hands over my head. 'So, everyone knew that –'

'Are you poisoned?' she says.

Fuck.

'No. I'm alright.'

'I think … I believe you,' she says. I feel her hand reach for mine in the darkness. She touches it lightly like she's testing something, then pulls it away. It's so small and warm, I feel bad all over again for having hit her.

I say, 'So what are you doing out here on your own?'

'I have escaped, too.'

'From where?'

There's quiet and she shifts a little closer. 'Were they looking for you …' she says, 'the helicopters?'

'I don't know.'

'Will they catch you?'

'They've gone.'

'They will come back maybe?'

'I don't want to be here to find out.'

'Ben,' she gets to her feet. 'Men are looking for me. Men are coming for me.'

'Who? What men? You mean the helicopters? Why would they −?'

'No. Not. These men want to take me back to where I was.'

'And that's not good?'

'I have to go. Good luck,' she says, and again I feel the brush of her palm on my hand.

'Wait, listen. You can't see a thing. Why don't you wait till morning?'

She stops and is still for a minute, then she says softly, 'They're coming.'

As soon as the words are out of her mouth, I hear it. It's faint at first but getting closer. Noises moving through the trees towards us. And suddenly, a yellow shaft of distant torchlight crosses her face and I see she's just a child. She must be all of twelve. A fringe of glossy black hair, and her eyes − they're a kind of violet blue. There's a bruise on her cheek that I'm hoping isn't from me. She looks terrified.

I pull up and grab her hand. 'Come on then.'

All we can do is run from the sounds. We stop every so often to listen, then force out into the darkness. At one point she whispers, 'Take off your shoes. It's quieter.'

I do as she says, tie them round my neck with the laces and, although it hurts and I'm scared of snakes, running barefoot makes sense. We go faster, ducking under mossy branches, brushing through ferns. Then we stop again. We're both breathing hard.

There's the faintest lick of dawn light across the sky. 'Can you hear them?' I say.

She shakes her head. 'Listen,' she says, 'water.'

There's a low clatter of water on stones to my right. As the sky lightens, we can see our way across moss-covered boulders and a thick mesh of ferns towards the sound. White water from a high, rocky outcrop tumbles past us on its way down the mountain. All we have to do now is follow it. But I need a drink. I slide over rocks, kneel in the river, drop my head and drink. It's sweet and clear and so cold it hurts my teeth. I drink my fill and all the time she's watching from the bank. She wears a rough woollen jacket, and red, wide-legged trousers that are too big and too short for her.

Every so often she turns to look back the way we came. Her blue eyes are wide in her pale face and she bites down on her fingers.

I wade over. 'So what do they want with you, these men?'

She slides down in front of me and stands at the edge, watching the rushing water. 'We must cross the river.'

When we haul up on the opposite bank, shivering, our clothes heavy with water-weight, she stops, breathing hard but not moving, and stares back at the way we went.

'Hey?' I say.

She rubs her cheeks with her sleeve. I crouch beside her. 'OK. Come on, quickly – tell me why you're running away. What do they want? If it's not to do with the camp … with the … *poison*, then –'

But she shakes her head, looks up at me. I try again. 'OK, OK. Not the camp. So … did you do something bad? Take something?' She shakes her head violently at that. And then I realise I'm being a total idiot. 'They want *you*?'

Slowly she nods. 'To take me back.'

'Back where?'

She whispers, 'City.'

'What city?'

'I don't know.'

'Where are you from?'

'I was born in a village. Far away.'

'So how did you –?'

'Mother and father dead – I had nowhere to go. No one to help me. I walked and walked and begged. Then … there was … a lady. She was kind to me – looked after me – but one day, men came and took me from her. Took me to the city.'

She pauses to wring water from the hem of her jacket, looks at me. 'That lady was not kind – she tricked me. She sold me.'

'Shit,' I say under my breath. 'What were you doing in the city … I mean, what did they –?' And as soon as I've asked it, her expression tells me all I need to know.

She squats down beside me and starts picking bits of leaf litter from between her toes. 'The man who bought me – he gave a lot of money. That is why he want me back. I was good for money. My eyes. You see? They're blue.'

I stare at her. 'Fuck.'

'We must go.'

'Where will you go?'

'I have aunt in Menghai. I think she will help me.'

'Where's that?'

She just points. And I guess that's what she's done. Just headed out from the city and followed her feet and that's what she'll go on doing until she gets there.

I stand and pull her up. 'Come on then. Let's go. If we follow the river, it'll take us somewhere we can both get help.'

She nods, her blue eyes brimming.

We travel along the course of the river, running where it's flat. And after a while, the ground begins to level out and it gets easier. I put my shoes back on.

We come to a rutted trail – caterpillar tracks in compacted mud – and, keeping in the shadow of the trees, we run. She's quick, her bare feet spin across the hard ground and it's all I can do to keep up. She doesn't look back.

I call out to her: 'Yun!! Yun! Stop a minute. You don't know where –'

She slows and turns. But she's not looking at me. She's looking beyond me, up the trail. I'm bent double, a fierce burning in my throat and chest, but I follow her gaze. Way off in the distance is a truck – a pick-up – it comes hurtling towards us out of the forest, throwing up a film of dust behind it. I can just make out two men standing in the back, naked from the waist up.

'Shit!'

She stamps her foot. 'Ben. Come! Come! Quick!'

I straighten up and I'm running again – after her and away from the truck. It's closing now and I catch up, grab her and pull her back into the forest where it's harder for them to follow.

I hear the brakes and the slam of the backboard and they're on foot now, coming after us fast. I look back once and see the front runner, his face contorted in a furious leer. I'm ahead now, and Yun's close on my heels but she's no match for him. I pull her to me, hoist her over my shoulder, turn, and charge away into the deep cover of the trees. She lets herself go limp and bends into me as I run. At my back I can hear them calling to each other in breathless barks.

It's raining now. Hard. Fat drops that stab my skin and my eyes. I run on blindly, holding Yun against me, until it all stops. I run headlong into the trunk of a tree and I'm knocked back with such force that I'm winded. At once, Yun's pulling at me, calling, 'Come on! Come Ben!'

A gun shot smacks out into the forest followed by the beating of a thousand wings. 'Ben! Ben! Please!' she calls.

I roll on to my side and try to stop the cramping in my chest. But by the time I'm breathing easier, it's too late. I smell them before I see them: sweat and gun metal, and then they're on us – dark shapes behind sheets of rain. I hear Yun's voice cry out. Someone kicks me in the stomach forcing the wind out of me a second time. At once, I feel that cold, black edge in me from a place I don't even know or understand, that cuts through the pain like a blade, and pushes me to my feet.

Yun's struggling between two of them, kicking and screaming. One holds her legs, the other her arms, and she hangs and wriggles between them, thrashing, twisting her head this way and that, her teeth bared.

I could run – leave it. Leave her. I don't owe her. I don't owe anyone anything. I'm all paid up on that.

But I stay.

There's a guy standing apart from the others. He's small and wiry, and I pick him. He's quick but not quick enough. I throw a punch and he falls back and I follow through with a well-aimed kick. I run at the man who has Yun by her arms, and head-butt him hard in the side. As he falls back, the pistol in his belt falls to the floor and I dive for it.

I point it at the guy still holding Yun by her ankles – the last man on his feet.

'Let her go. Now.' He looks at me, then behind me, then back at me.

'Let. Her. Go.'

Nothing. He tightens his grip on her and his mouth breaks into a sort of smirk.

I start to raise the gun, my finger on the cold loop of the trigger. But I'm bluffing. I hesitate, and in that moment the man I floored leaps up and runs at me.

It all happens so fast.

The gun goes off and I stagger back under the force of it.

Then everything slows down.

There's a moment before he falls when his chest seems to open like a flower and a red spray washes into the rain and runs to the ground. I watch him, the blood on his shirt as he sinks down. The pistol is still in my hand. My fist closes around the cold-hot weight of it.

I look at the others on the ground. They shrink from me, flat palms held upwards. I bring the gun up again.

'Ben!' Yun's voice pulls me back. She tugs on my shirt but I can't go yet. I'm looking at the man I shot. He lies on his back, a froth of blood and spittle at the corner of his mouth as he coughs out his last breath and is still, his eyes fixed and milky.

I look back at the others and they're watching me watching him. One of them, the younger of the two, moves to get up, and I ready the gun but I let it hang in my hand for a fraction of a moment and his friend springs at me, grabs it, and hits me across the jaw. I go down and in two seconds flat, there's a gun in my face and Yun is screaming.

I push up on my elbows and face him. I'm wet to the bone. We all are. Behind him I can see Yun being carried away towards the road, a flash of red, bucking and screaming. The man with me cocks the gun and narrows his eyes. But I'm not going to die here.

Yun's cries are fading now and we're alone. I look at him. He's not much older than me. There are tight, silver scars on his chest and neck.

I have an idea. I say, 'Money? You want money?'

He stares at me.

'You speak English?' I say. 'You want money?'

He nods slowly. 'English. Yes.'

'I have money. I'll give you money. For me and the girl. You let us go.'

Very slowly I reach into my shirt. The envelope he gave me is there, wet and pulpy. I show him the contents. 'Dollars. You want?'

Holding the cash, I kneel, then stand up. Slowly. Watching him all the time. His eyes are on the envelope but his knuckles are tight over the gun.

'Give me,' he says. 'The money. Give it to me.'

I stand my ground. 'Drop the gun.'

And we stand there in the rain. We could be waiting for a gig to start, drinking a beer. And as suddenly as it started, the rain stops, and at once there's bright sunlight and birdsong, and I can feel myself starting to sweat again. The man I shot lies on the ground a little way off, his body steams in the wet heat.

I hold out my hand. 'The gun. Drop it.'

He looks back to where the other one went with Yun. Wet leaves glisten and the forest hums around us. He lifts the gun and aims it at me but his hand is trembling, his body taut. And he throws it. Hurls it away from us both. It clatters against a rock and there's a tiny shower of sparks.

'Money,' he says.

'For both of us. You take the money. You let us go. Yes?'

He takes the envelope and peels out the wet notes.

'A thousand dollars. You understand? US dollars. Now go and get me the girl.'

He pockets the cash, turns, and trudges away toward the track, head down. I follow close behind him. Soon we see the truck. His friend stands beside it, holding a semi-automatic rifle. There's no sign of Yun.

Before I have a chance to decide just what I'm going to do, my guy with the money takes off suddenly at a run in the opposite direction. The other man shouts and fires at him. A yelp of pain and he goes down. And bank notes fly up and fall like leaves over the forest floor. I dive for cover and wait, and his howls fill the air.

Silence. I crouch down, cover my head, my ears are ringing and my chest is tight. The heat bears down on my neck and shoulders and I close my eyes and I can see the body of the man I shot. What the bullet I fired had done to him. It's like I can see inside that hole in his chest – like I can crawl in there where it's still warm – see the thick blue veins, and the branching of bone like china …

'Get up!' I open my eyes and the man is standing over me holding the rifle. 'GET UP!'

With my hands over my head I do as he says. He slams the barrel at my back and I walk.

2

I'm lying face down on ridged metal in the back of the truck, my hands and feet are bound and I'm half-covered with a tarpaulin. There's a smell of diesel and wet rope. I'm wedged against the side of the truck on one side, and on the other, something soft but solid, and when I can inch my head to face it, I see it's the bodies of the dead men. Their skin's drying and their eyes are white in their sockets.

'Ben?' A small voice against the angry rumble of the engine.

'Yun?' There's a pause and a shuffling. 'You OK?' I say.

'I'm OK.' She sounds flat and broken.

'Who are they?'

'They work for the man who paid for me.'

Silence.

My face is still near the floor but I can twist to see her over the bodies. She's lying on her side, her hands bound behind her, like me.

'I tried to give them money, one of them,' I say softly. 'A thousand dollars – so they'd let us go, but –'

I hear her breathing. Shallow and sharp.

'Thank you. But –'

'What?' I can't feel my face on one side any more. And then I realise she's crying.

'I think … I think that would not work.'

'But –'

'They will make many more money than that from me.'

'Yeah. Yeah. Fuck. I'm sorry.'

'I am sorry. Because of me you will not get home.'

I go for a wry laugh and find I'm dribbling. 'Look. It's not over yet. We'll find a way to get out. I'm still alive. I'm strong … I can –'

'You know why they take you too?'

'You mean, why they didn't –?'

'Why you are still alive?'

A great gaping hole opens up inside me as I consider all the possibilities. And anything and everything I can think of begins and ends with me never getting out of China. Never getting home. I push my skull into the metal ridges and say slowly, 'Why?'

'Money also,' she says.'

'What?'

'Can make money from you, same as me.'

The truck hits a rut in the track and bounces. I hear the driver curse in the cab. The bodies roll towards

me, squashing me against the side of the truck. There's
nothing more from Yun.

After a while, the driver pulls over and gets out. The
dank tarpaulin is stretched right over us, and the ground
is smoother after that. I guess we're on the motorway.
But in my head I'm a million miles away.

In my room at the camp, when the siren sounded
in the morning, the picture that would fire into my
muddled brain on waking was always the same. I got
good at shoving it away. I could squash it so effectively
that within seconds I'd be back in the present.

I owned that picture. But I kept it caged like a
mad dog.

The picture was Sophy. Her hair in strands on the
pillow, her slim fingers opening her shirt, her smiling
up at me when I'd kissed her. And I let it out now. I
let it run around my head.

I'm coming back to you, Sophy. Whatever you're
doing, wherever you are.

I sleep then, or at least that's how it seems. And when
I wake, it's darker. We've been travelling for hours. Yun
is silent next to me and the dead bodies are starting
to reek. It's so hot, my breath under the tarpaulin is
condensing.

I call, 'Yun? Yun? Are you OK?' but there's no answer.
I rock myself and force my body onto its side.

'Yun?'

A groan from a little way off.

'Yun!'

'Ben?'

'It's me. Are you OK?'

There's a long pause, and I hear the effort it's taking her just to whisper: 'Water. I need to drink.'

I start to make a noise – to make him stop. Drumming against the bed of the truck with my feet and hands until it bumps to a stop. I hear the door slam and footsteps on the tarmac behind me. The sound of traffic slicing past us never stops. We must be close to the city.

The tailboard's released and he's in the back, pulling off the tarp. He gives me a half-hearted kick and I roll onto my front. 'Water,' I say, 'we need water.'

He mutters something under his breath, jumps down, and I hear the door of the cab go. After some time, he's back with a bottle. I can just turn my head to see him lift Yun's limp body and pour water into her mouth. She's like a rag doll, her tongue lolls to one side and her face is pale. Water dribbles from her open mouth but I see her revive a little. He squats down and pinches her cheeks. She comes to and spits at him and he rocks back on his haunches and laughs.

'Hey!' I say. 'I want some. Give me some.'

In answer, he gets up and comes and stands over me holding the bottle. His hair's long and the skin on his face is pitted and thick. He unscrews the cap, and looking at me all the time, he pours the lot onto the floor just inches from my face. Just in between me and the body of the boy he shot. It pools for a moment then runs away. I force myself to say nothing and I turn my head into the floor again.

Darkness then as the tarp is pulled back into place. He guns the engine and we're moving out into traffic. Slower this time, stopping and starting.

'Ben?' Yun whispers. I hear her at the edges of my consciousness but I'm losing it. I'm swimming. I'm diving in water away from the heat, and it's black and cold where I'm going and I'm holding my breath.

Water. Cold water. All over me. Bright lights and the rush of water wake me, and I come back again. Coughing and spluttering. I open my eyes and another man is there: a fat Chinese guy wearing a greasy apron. He's pouring water on me from a tin bucket. He bends over me and pulls me into a sitting position with my back to the cab. My head's hammering and my wrists and ankles are numb.

He unties me and lets me drink from the bucket, holding it in his beefy arms. I feel it rush into me, cold and sharp, and the shock of it makes me gasp. I look for Yun but she's gone. The bodies too.

'Where is she? The girl? Where is she?'

He shrugs at me, wags a fat finger. His head is covered in gristly scabs and he smells bad. From somewhere I can hear dogs barking.

'Up,' he says. I look up at him and he gestures with his thumb. 'Up!' I want to stand up but I can't. My body's locked itself down or locked me inside it.

He lurches into me, and in one heave, I'm swaying in front of him. He dips into my stomach and I'm bucked up over his shoulder where I lie like corpse as he descends from the back of the truck. The sound of traffic goes, and we're inside somewhere – concrete floor and a smell of raw meat. He pushes me onto a chair, kneels down, and starts to rub some kind of grease into my ankles. It's gooey, and smells like drain cleaner but I can feel the blood beginning to flow again. He's hard at work, pummelling my feet, when I lift my head and look at where I am.

We're in a kind of warehouse. It's long and low with strip lighting in the metal rafters. Wooden pallets are stacked at one end, and there's a door leading off near where I'm sitting. And as I look, it opens.

Two men walk in. One is the guy that brought us here, the other is a small Chinese man in a dark suit. He looks smart, like he's in charge. His shoes snap across the concrete floor towards me. He barks something and my fat friend heaves himself up and shuffles backwards into the shadows.

For a long time, the small man stands and looks at me. Every so often he brings a handkerchief up to his face and dabs around his mouth. The other guy leans in and there's something in his hand. Something white and ridged: a surgical mask.

I get to my feet, step back, looking for the exit. I'm thinking I could make a run for it but before I can do anything, the fat guy is on me like he knew exactly what I was thinking, clamping my arms in a sweaty hug. The small man is busy pulling the mask over his nose and mouth.

I let myself be pushed back on to the chair with the fat guy standing over me. The small man clip-clops up to me. He's wearing heels. His breathing in the mask is amplified. The other guy stands close, a rag over his face.

The small man motions to Fat Boy to keep me still, and he comes up close. He says something in Mandarin, and Fat Boy opens my shirt and wrenches it off me.

The little man studies me then. He looks at my eyes, my teeth; he taps my chest and listens to my breathing. He points at my arms – at the thin red tracks where the needles did their work in the lab.

'Smack?'

I look at him.

'Junk? Heroin? You a junkie?'

I shake my head. 'Medicine.'

He steps back, his hand holding the mask in place. 'You sick?'

'I'm … no … I'm not sick. Where's Yun? Where's the girl?'

He ignores me. 'You are English? American?'

'English. Where's –?'

'You sick? Hot? Here?' And he puts a neat little hand across his forehead then under his arm. His nails are filed in points.

I stare at him. I'm trying hard to figure out what exactly is going on. And whether I should say I'm sick so they'll maybe let me go, or whether it's better to say I'm not so they don't kill me. I decide to stick with being well.

'I'm not sick. Where's the girl?'

He smiles and looks back at the others. They nod and shuffle on their feet.

'You stand up now. Get up!'

Fat Boy pulls me up by my shoulders and I stand in front of the man. I close my eyes for a moment and there are spinning lights in the black. I want to throw up. He tips back and forward on his little heels and puts a hand against my chest. Cold and wet. Thin fingertips over my ribs. I try to move but Fat Boy won't let me. The little man takes my hand and closes it into a fist.

'You big boy. Lot of muscle. You like to fight?'

I say nothing. Sophy's in my head. I can smell her. Feel her. And, like always, my father.

He walks around me and stops. He brushes down my back with his hand. 'Snake. Very good sign in China. Very good. You good sign for me.'

He comes back to face me, waves a hand and Fat Boy pushes me back into my chair. 'You have rest tonight. Eat. Drink. Tomorrow we see about fighting.' He nods and starts for the door.

'Fuck you,' I say. They turn.

I'm on my feet now. Fat Boy's looking worried.

'Whatever it is, I'm not doing it,' I say. 'You can't keep me here.'

'You. Not. Doing?' He says the words slowly, then his voice rises to a shrill squeak: 'You doing! I tell you. You do. Two of my men killed by you – because of you – you owe me. I own you, English boy.'

Fat Boy gives me a flabby backhander that sends me flying across the floor. My teeth are buzzing and my nose is bleeding but I get back up and I run at him. I go for his belly and head-butt him. He staggers back, winded and wheezing.

'Yes. You very good,' says the man. 'Very good. You will make a good show. Plenty money! Pay back for my dead men.' I look at him. He's smiling. He pulls a gun from his pocket, jerks it at me, and I move. I walk and he follows, and the gun stays inches from my skull.

I'm coming back to you Sophy.

3

Sophy

The air in here's like jam. I lean over, open my window and suck in the night air. There are lights in the distance from the army trucks and the braziers by the road blocks. There's a faint warmth in the night sometimes – the last dregs of the summer. The leaves are turning, and for the first time in ages, I feel sort of like I'm coming back. For so long, I've felt like whatever thread it was that joined me to the rest of the world had broken. And it's nothing to do with what's happened. It's like I said, I just fell through a door – through a crack in the earth – and I couldn't come back.

He's alive. He's alive. He's alive. I whisper it over and over in my throat till it's dry. And as I pull the early morning air into my lungs, I let myself smile. I actually smile. And you have to believe me when I say I haven't done that in forever. I can let myself think about him. Want him. And it feels so good and so bad at the same time. A whole year has passed since I told him I loved him. So much has happened, so much has changed.

I've changed for a start. I don't expect anything anymore. Don't wish for anything. Every day is just like the last one. It's like I've shrunk to the size of a small insect and I'm very, very slowly crawling through coarse grass, except all the time, although I'll never know it, I'm getting closer and closer to the edge of some great cliff. And one day I'll just fall, be blown out to sea on the wind. Blown into pieces. Into nothing.

If he's alive, if he's survived this far, I know he'll do it: that whatever's happened, he'll find a way to find me again.

I don't know how I do it but I make myself wait till 8.00 am, then I call Charlie. And as usual, it takes about sixteen attempts before I get a connection. He's moving when he answers it. I can hear his breath coming in short bursts. There's noise in the background – shouting – and he's shouting over it down the phone. 'Hey. Sophy! Long time no speak. How you doing?'

And I can't say it straight away. I have to hold it close a bit longer. Keep it ... 'I'm good. What's going on there?'

'Food riot. Poor fuckers. Two lorries. A thousand people. They're taking the place apart. I can't really talk now. I can call you later. But you're OK, yeah?'

'Er ... Yeah. Yeah. I just wanted to –'

There's a shout and sounds of a scuffle up close. I hear him shouting: 'Move back! Move back.' And then: 'Listen, Sophy, I'll call you later. OK?' And he's gone, and I'm left whispering the words I wanted him to hear: 'He's alive.'

He won't tell me but I think Charlie's in London. I know it's everywhere but London's the worst. That was where it started. They keep the news fairly tight but everyone knows, everyone knows how it happens – how it starts – with a fever, a rash, how you lose your mind – but by then it's too late because your blood, even your saliva, is infectious. They say it eats you up from the inside. The first person to get it was dead in days. He wandered into St Mary's in Paddington covered in lumps, shouting and screaming and foaming at the mouth, and of course nobody knew what it was, then the lumps just burst open – just split – then two nurses got it, and a doctor, and a load of other people he'd been in contact with. And quickly, so quickly, cases started appearing all over: in Europe, in New York, in San Francisco. It's only a matter of time before it's all over the world. When the radio works, which isn't often, they tell us they're close to finding a vaccine – a cure – but everyone knows that's a load of crap.

When we get the internet, there's new stuff every day, talking about the latest mad cures. Some people have gone totally medieval: someone reckons boiling dandelion flowers will do it; another person claims blood letting works. *Leeches*? In the 21st century? But of course the only way to really stay safe is to stay away from other people. Completely. And that's got to be hard at any age but I'm nearly 19 and it's driving me crazy. Actually insane. Certifiable.

Everyone's scared. I'm scared. Mum and Dad argue all the time. I don't think Lily really knows what's going on – just that she can't play out with her friends any more. Dad's ripped up the patio and his crap, cheapo hot tub, and planted vegetables. Potatoes. Everyone's done it. All down the street. He sits out most nights with a carving knife, watching for anyone trying to break in over the fence. That blade's so sharp it would cut through bone.

So we're stuck. The schools are closed, churches, shops – anywhere there's a chance of meeting other people. There's no public transport. Docks and airports are shut so there's not much food or fuel. We sterilize everything. We can't go anywhere, and even if we had the petrol, which we don't, the town's totally locked down. There are roadblocks on all the roads out of town and army patrols at the end of every road. People are going crazy with fear and waiting. A woman up the road has got religion big time. She broadcasts passages from the Bible through a loudhailer from her bedroom window.

Today's different though – for me anyway – today I have to get out. Just to walk around. I'm so filled up with the news, I can't sit still.

I grab a mask and dunk it in fluid. I'm used to it now but the smell used to make me gag. It's like a bitter kind of aniseed that gets in your nose and eyes and mouth.

Mum's in the garden, bent over a row of greens, and Dad's lying on the floor in the sitting room watching DVD's of old football games. We get power on and off these days but it's best in the mornings.

He lifts his head as I pass. 'Where d'you think you're going?'

'Out.'

He pushes up on his elbows. 'No. No. No way. That's not happening. There's been a case. Town centre. Jim was on the CB this morning. No way.'

'I don't care.'

OK. So this is not the way to pacify someone with the shortest fuse in the western world and a predisposition to behave like a total Nazi but I really, really don't care. I can be scared and lonely sitting in my room, or scared and lonely on the street, and today I'm restless as hell and no one – not even him – is going to stop me.

'Oh, you don't care? Great! Charming! Fabulous! You hear that, Anne?' he calls. 'She doesn't care? Doesn't care that she's going to be bringing a dose of this thing right to our door?'

Mum comes in, wiping her hands on her apron. She looks a state. She used to look after herself. Highlights once a month, pedicure, now she looks like some Home-Front housewife from the Second World War: hair tied up in a scarf, rubber boots, no make up.

'Sophy, love. *Please*?' she says.

'No good appealing to her better nature, she hasn't got one,' he says. 'Selfish and spoiled. That's what we're looking at. That's what we're dealing with. Don't you ever listen to the broadcasts? Read the leaflets? This is a major epidemic. Worldwide … there is no –'

'Martin, *please*?'

'Martin, please, *what*? Don't interrupt me. You're no better: talking to neighbours. The only way to beat this thing is lockdown. Shut down. Doors and windows, and stay inside until –'

'Martin –'

'I will NOT be interrupted! DO YOU HEAR ME?'

Suddenly the TV fizzes and the screen goes black. I hear the rattle of the fridge closing down.

'Fuck!' he says.

I turn and walk up the hall and close the front door quietly behind me. I'm two doors down the street and I can still hear them. I know he has a point but I'll never admit that to him. It's been months now that we've been living on top of each other in that house. Falling over each other, snapping and carping. And every day there's something: a new cluster of the virus in a new place; some 'new' cure and new government flyers through the letter box, screaming, "Keep Your Family Safe."

But nothing's working. Nothing's changing. It's getting worse. I know it. We all know it. And that's why we're annoying the hell out of each other. We're all scared.

We're terrified.

There's a steady drizzle outside. A few stubborn patches of snow cling to piles of rubbish along the street. I walk to the end and stare beyond the blocks. A soldier in riot gear stands guard, his elbows on the barricade. I get closer.

'Hey,' I say.

He looks up. 'Hey,' then: 'Sophy? Is that you under there?'

I pull down my mask. 'Josh? I don't believe it! How's it going?'

He laughs and lets up his face guard. I recognise him from school. He used to have spots but they're fading now and his skin is marked with little pink pits where they used to be. He's got nice eyes. He did English with me.

'What can I say?' he says. 'Shit. You know. Just shit. Business as usual.'

'Is it true about – has there been outbreak here, in town?'

He shrugs, looks down. Something in the way he holds himself reminds me of Ben. 'No one tells me anything,' he says. 'What have you been up to?'

'Well … let me see …' I drag it out. I'm playing, but he's listening. 'I would have to say, I'm doing … absolutely nothing. Yeah. That's it. Nothing at all. I'm doing less than nothing – apart from going mad. Steadily losing my mind.'

He stares at me, dark brown eyes unblinking. And then he puts a hand on my arm. Just for a moment.

And he's wearing protective gloves but it feels so good to be touched, to feel another person, that I have to hold my breath to stop from crying right there at this stupid road block, with Josh from my English class. And then it makes me think of Ben and how I told him I loved him. And I have to turn away for a second. There's a dead dog on the road, its limbs twisted and stiff, its mouth open. They shoot them. This thing can cross species. All the leaflets tell you that. I'd walked straight past it.

'You'll be OK. Just got to hang in there.'

'Yeah. Yeah. I know. I'll be fine.'

'I heard the Americans are close to a vaccine,' he says. He's smiling.

'Me too,' I say, 'And that it's carried by moles. You don't believe it do you, the vaccine stuff – it's all bulllshit.'

He shrugs. 'Yeah. I guess you're right. Got to hold on to something – even bullshit feels OK after this long.' There's a kind of awkward quiet between us for a minute and then he goes and asks, 'Did you ever hear anything about Ben – about what happened?'

I look at him. I want to tell someone. Why not him? I nod slowly – I can feel myself starting to cry again. My eyes are prickling. I take a breath. He's looking at me intently.

He shifts his rifle across to his other arm. 'Really?' he says.

Again I nod. 'Just this morning. Someone called me. I don't who … and she said he's … he's … I think he's alive. He's in China.'

And I'm sobbing out the last words, groping up my sleeve for a tissue. Josh hesitates a moment then lifts up the barrier tape gingerly and comes over. He goes for a tame little pat on the shoulder first, then when I don't shrug him off, which was maybe what he was scared of, he puts his arm around me and I cry into his chest like I haven't cried in months.

'Hey, hey, Sophy. It's OK. That's good news right? Isn't it? I mean … he's alive, he's OK?'

'I can't … I can't … I just can't … hold on to it. You know?' I pull back sniffling and I see his Kevlar vest is wet with my tears. I loop my hair back and wipe my face. There's a lick of hair across my cheek and before I can hook it back, he's there. He lifts it so gently, tucking it behind my ear that it sets me off again. 'I'm sorry. I'm sorry. It's just you're being so nice, and this thing, this thing … about Ben. I mean it's so great, and I thought it was everything I wanted and it is. It is. It really is, but I don't know what to do with it. It's like I can't hold it all in my head. It's so … so …'

'Big?'

I manage a smile. 'Am I crazy? Do I sound like an idiot?'

And he's nice enough to say: 'No. You don't sound like an idiot. Not at all. I get you. It's like you've heard he's alive but that's like the tip of the iceberg. I mean, you don't know where he is or how to get to him, or how he's going to get to you. You don't whether he's … he might be …'

And he leaves it there but we both know what he means: Ben might be sick. The girl didn't know. Maybe she hadn't understood. I haven't heard of any cases in the Far East. But who knows? And besides she hadn't said when she'd last seen him. You get this thing and you're dead in days. Josh is right – it's big. It's huge.

'Thanks, Josh. I'm really sorry. You must think I'm –'

'No. No, I don't.' An army truck pulls up and he's distracted for a minute. Quickly he steps back behind the tape.

'It was nice to talk to you,' I say, but he's looking the other way. Two men in full Level 4 biohazard gear are coming towards him. I push my mask back on, go to walk back the way I've come. Down the street, past the dog. They'll collect it this evening with the others.

'Sophy!' Josh calls.

He leaves the others and comes towards me. He looks nervous. He lowers his voice, says quickly, 'Listen, it's true about the outbreak. They think they've contained it but tell your family to stay safe. But, I … if … Oh fuck – what I mean is, if you want a shoulder, you know … I'm at the end of the road till next week. Then we're being sent somewhere else, I think.' He tries for a smile but it doesn't happen.

I look at him. 'Thanks for telling me. And … I'd really like that. To see you. It'll give me something to look forward to.'

He studies my face. 'You being sarcastic?'

'*What*? No! Christ, Josh, talking to you has been the best thing I've done in forever. I promise.'

'Shit, sorry. Not used to … OK. I'm off. I'll see you, I hope?'

I nod and wave him off and he thuds back towards the block where the other two are waiting.

I go home and Mum and Dad are still arguing. He's on his feet and they're kind of circling the sitting room like a pair of wild cats. Lily's sitting at the table with her chin in her hands, staring into space. She looks pale and the rims of her eyes are red.

'You OK, piglet?' I ask.

She nods but she doesn't look so good.

'Don't mind about Mum and Dad. They don't mean it really. Come on. Let's play a game.'

She rubs her eyes and nods.

By the evening she's screaming and writhing and clutching her head. Her eyes are red and streaming and Mum and Dad have stopped shouting at each other and Dad's picking up the phone.

4

Eggs. Fried eggs and rice in a small bowl topped with tangled rings of chilli. Fat Boy, whose name is Lee, is sitting on the one chair in the room they put me in. He's picking at the scabs on his head and he's smiling. I'm on a thin mattress on a stone floor. I slept fitfully last night and woke in a cold sweat just before dawn.

There's a high narrow window on the wall, and a thin bar of sunlight grazes the floor. I've got no idea where I am. The tracks on my arms are inflamed and my head's pounding. Behind the wall, there's what sounds like someone pissing into a bucket. Voices raised and stilled and raised again.

The bowl is hot and steaming in my hands and I eat, shaping the rice into parcels in my fingers and lifting them into my mouth like we did at the camp. When I'm done, he motions to me to stand and he locks me in a kind of sweaty embrace that nearly lifts me off my feet.

'Come, come on, English boy.'

He unlocks the door and leads me out of the room into a long corridor with a torn linoleum floor. All along the corridor there are doors like mine, some locked, some not. He pads along, with me following him, to the end of the corridor where he stops outside a double door. I hear sharp grunts and slamming noises from the other side. I hang back a bit but he closes his chubby thumb and forefinger around my wrist in a tweezer-grip and pulls me through the door.

The room's low and poorly lit; it smells of ripe sweat and leather. Punch bags hang from the ceiling like giant chrysalids, and in the centre is a sprung ring surrounded on all sides by a high mesh fence – a cage.

Two boys of about my age are inside it, dancing around each other, their fists up. They wear shorts. Their heads are shaved and they're bare-chested, and the skin on their backs and chests is a patchwork of faded tattoos and pinkish scars. I notice their shins are split and bloody. The small guy from last night is sitting in an upright chair a little way off, watching them, a thick bamboo cane resting on his lap. The man who brought me here stands next to him nodding. Now and again, the small man claps his hands together, pointing at his chin, and every time he does this, the boys stop what they're doing and glance at him anxiously. He waves them on and the dance starts up again.

The bamboo cane is streaked with blood.

They look like they're fighting but they're not. They're just moving around each other, eye to eye, fist to fist. Their hands are bandaged.

I turn to Lee. 'What are they doing?'

He chuckles and whacks me on the back with a force that pulses down my spine into my knees. 'Mr Ping like to watch. They training – get ready to fight. Get strong legs. Toes. Heels. Very good.'

And he mimes hitting at my legs with a cane.

Ping is on his feet now and walking around the cage. Again they stop but he snaps his fingers and they resume. I know he's seen me now. He's showing off – showing me himself – the power he has. That this is his place and what happens in here is down to him. He turns and fixes his eyes on me and barks a command at the boys. And he keeps looking at me, as if gauging my reaction to what's happening in the cage.

The boys are in to each other now: kicking, punching, pulling and biting. In the mouth of one I see a flash of teeth filed into points like a cat's. He has a tattoo of a rooster on his neck and the rooster's crowing and its neck is elongated and reaches up to the boy's ear.

He's getting the upper hand, ramming his opponent against the cage. And when he drops him, the boy's skin is etched with the criss-cross pattern of the fence. He staggers to his feet but he's not ready, and the other bounces back and knees him sharply in the chest. I don't look away and I keep my face blank.

The boy has dropped to the floor. His nose looks broken and there are bite marks on his chest. Mr Ping picks up the bamboo cane and with the pointed end, pushes and pokes at the boy through the mesh, screaming at him. I watch as he drives the stick into a cut on the boy's neck. The boy howls in pain and tries to twist away; clawing towards the centre of the ring but there's no escape. The bamboo cane reaches for him, corkscrewing into his flesh. The one with the rooster tattoo stands back watching, breathing hard. And then as Mr Ping gives his opponent a final twist, looks over at me – right at me – bares his shark teeth. The man with Ping unlocks the cage and Rooster jumps down, swigs from a bottle of water, swills it around his mouth and spits it on the floor by my feet. He's probably my age but close up, his skin's hard like hide and I wonder just how long he's been here. A sick feeling creeps over me and I grit my teeth not to let it show.

Lee shakes his head, blinks at me, and I stare back at him. The room goes quiet and he says slowly and carefully, his eyes on Ping: 'Sanshou, kick-box, ju jitsu, use all style. Mix up. He was watching other boy. He read him, use all part of body. Stab with shin, elbow … you can do this?'

I fold my arms over my chest. Keep staring.

'This is Chang,' he says, pointing at the Rooster. 'You will fight this boy. First fight … Come, come.' And he trots over to the cage where Mr Ping is standing holding the long bamboo prod. Lee heaves himself into the cage, picks up the defeated boy and carries him out. The boy's too weak to stand and blood is crusting all down his neck and chest. Mr Ping whispers something to his man and watches approvingly as the man ties the injured boy by his wrists and hoists the rope over a hook in the ceiling. He secures it and the boy hangs there, his feet swinging off the ground and his head lolling to one side. His feet are tattooed with roses, climbing on thorny vines up from his toes.

Lee looks at me and swallows. His face is drained.

Mr Ping holds a handkerchief to his face as he talks to me. 'Let me see you work,' he says. 'Hit him.'

I shake my head. 'No.'

He smiles, dabs at his face with the handkerchief.

'I'm not doing it,' I say.

Lee whispers: 'He don't stop. You do what he say. Must.'

Rooster shuffles and twitches, and the boy lifts his head a moment and opens one eye. I turn to leave but the other man catches and holds me. There's a gun in his hand.

'You do what he say,' Lee repeats. 'He don't stop.'

'I told you, I'm not doing it.'

I hear the gun cock close to my head. 'Hit him,' Ping urges, 'hit this boy.'

The boy's eyes flicker up at me and roll back white in his head. I feel sick and sad and raging at the same time, and I don't know what I'm going to do – I don't trust myself to do anything because I think if I start I won't ever stop.

And then Rooster's there. Like he was going to do it anyway.

He pulls back his fist and hits the boy square in the stomach, and he buckles and hangs limp from the hook. Rooster steadies himself, then goes in again – one more time – I hear the crunch of bone on bone as the boy's ribs give against his fist.

I feel cold. That blackness again: like a cold black mouth closing over me, swallowing me.

The boy's unconscious when the man takes him down, blood and spittle spooling from his mouth onto the floor. Mr Ping stands very still, arms tight against his sides, pinching the handkerchief in his left hand. He doesn't look at me. He says something to Lee, tucks the handkerchief in his top pocket, and leaves the room.

I turn my face away and vomit.

Lee pulls me up and I stand there heaving while he unlocks a door to the side and with a nod, ushers Rooster and me through and disappears back inside. After the gloom of the fighting room, the bright sunlight is a shock.

I try to say something to him but Rooster pushes past me and I stand on the step blinking. The building we're in leads out onto a scrubby lot surrounded by a high wire fence. Beyond the fence on all sides, are other, taller buildings, burned out from the inside: thick grey breeze block towers, shot with steel wires. I can hear the sound of fast-moving traffic in the distance, and it makes me think we're on some kind of industrial estate outside a town. Two chained Alsatians sprawl and scratch and pant in the heat. One of them looks up at me with cold yellow eyes as I pass.

About eight or nine boys are there lounging against the fence, smoking, some playing cards. They look up at me and nudge each other. Rooster walks over to the group and there's a shuffle as room is made for him to sit down. They cluster about him and he's showing his wounds – even from here I can see his knuckles are bleeding. I tuck myself in to the edge and watch. I can't get my breath yet – it's like my lungs are clogged with wool. I keep seeing it over, reaching for a reason – something that's going to make it OK – to make me OK again.

I try to see the small stuff – make myself look: the grains of parched earth that crumble to dust in your fingers; the way the fence mesh is charred and twisted; an ant making its way around a stone.

And when I'm ready, when I'm breathing again, I can look up.

The building we've come from looks like a disused army barracks: a long chain of low huts with corrugated roofs and high slits to let in light. There are bars against all the windows, and padlocks on every door. Closer, just over the fence, there's an enclosed space where several cars are parked, and beyond that, another fence. Expensive cars. As I watch, I see Lee come out with

the other man and approach the lot. Over his shoulder
he carries a long hessian sack. I walk up to get a closer
look. The sack is stained with dark patches. The other
man flicks a key and the boot of a large black BMW
opens. Lee shifts the bundle into his arms and lowers
it into the boot. The sack gapes for a moment and I
see clearly: a foot with dark roses curling up the ankle.

5

Bile in my throat. My chest tightens.

I've killed a man, watched another die, and now this. In as many days. As the car slams into gear and spins away from the lot, I turn and slide down the fence. I try to find Sophy but she's gone. All I can see behind my eyes is blood. The hole in the man's chest, the blood. And the boy hanging there, and a gun in my face, and that feeling like I could tear down buildings. Did I want it? In some dark, deep, secret part of me? Did Rooster cheat me out of something I was ready to do? I remember my father's words, the way he talked about his work. Dealing in death. Is that what I'm doing? Where I'm going? If I fight Rooster, will I want to kill him? Will I enjoy it?

What's happening to me?

There's very little talk in the yard. The boys play cards silently. A boy who looks younger than the rest of us whistles a solitary tune. He's missing an ear.

All are scarred in some way or another. All have the marks of home made tattoos. They stare at me but no one approaches. No one speaks to me. But like I say, they don't really seem talk to each other much. I wonder where Yun is and whether I'll ever see her again, and whether seeing her will help me make sense of what I've done. Someone, something, has to.

Later, I eat in my cell: rice, and what look like some kind of deep fried insect. Lee comes in later with a cut throat razor and shaves my head. He pats me and punches me in the stomach. 'Mr Ping want you to fight tonight, Ben – see how you handle yourself in the cage.'

'*What?*'

He acts like he's not heard it. 'Hold belly tight. Balls too,' he laughs. 'You kick with legs. With feet. Hard in balls,' he mimes the action. 'Ears. Nose. Mouth,' he shows me, pulling on his ear lobe, nose and hooking his fingers inside his lip and tugging.

I stare at him. 'What if I say no?'

His eyes are wide. 'Not again. Mr Ping very angry with you. He don't like this. You say no again, not good. Mr Ping want to see you fight.'

'This is nothing to do with me. It's not my fight – I don't have to –'

'Ben,' he says, 'you do not understand.'

'Understand what?'

'You cannot say no to him.'

'Yeah? I just did – back there.'

He shakes his head. 'No. *He* said yes – he let you say no.'

'I don't –'

'When you say no, he thinks – this boy is hard guy. Not afraid.'

'What? It was a *test*?'

He stares at me for a bit, then he says, 'You are a prisoner. Like me. Like Chang. You make trouble, you say no to this fight … then there is trouble for everyone.' He waits, looks at me again. 'He will kill you,' he says.

I look back at him and he looks so fucking earnest. I nod once and he nods and he breathes out. But I'm still holding my breath.

Thinking.

I'm not worth a lot. The only thing I have, the only reason I matter, is because of what I'm carrying in my blood, and if Ping shoots me before I have a chance to get out and do something with it, then I've messed up the only good my father ever did – the only thing he could ever set and square against the bad.

'Alright,' I say.

Lee looks down at my hands, takes one in his and grips it – he pinches the ends of my fingers, fishes in his back pocket and pulls out a nail file. I go to wrench away but he sits back on the chair and pulls me towards him. Frowning in concentration, he sets about filing my broken nails into jagged points.

'Is good, Ben. Is good! You like cat. Can do this.' He pulls my nails across his chest where they leave a spray of red weals. There's something about Lee that reminds me of Maurice. His smell. His relentless cheerfulness. From another pocket he pulls a chocolate bar in a grubby wrapper. He breaks it in two and offers me half. And again, I think of Maurice and his ginger nuts in the back of the shop. I take it.

'Thanks, Lee. The boy who was … who was hit – what happened to him?'

He shakes his head and tuts to himself. 'He not very strong.'

'Where is he?'

Again he shakes his head. 'Gone.'

I know what he means – I can't even say it. But I still stood there and watched it happen.

He fixes me with an unblinking stare. For a moment he looks like the saddest man on the planet.

'Why did Chang do it?' I say. 'Why did he hit the boy?'

He looks down, mutters something.

'*What*?' I say.

'I don't know.'

'He doesn't even know me – why would he –?

He rubs a finger along the file, up and down. 'We are all the same,' he says.

'But that was for me – Ping was testing me and he got in the way.'

He just looks at me.

I say, 'What'll happen to him?'

He waits a long time before answering. 'I don't know,' he says finally. He's getting up like he wants to close it down when I lean forward.

'And the girl? The girl I was with – what happened to her?'

He rouses himself, sniffs and spits. 'She is Mr Ping's girl. You want girl? Very bad before fight. After. If you win fight, I get you girl. Lee get you present of girl. Yes?'

'No. I don't mean that. I don't want ... I just ... Where is she?'

He hesitates and makes a great play of looking around him before replying. 'She belong to Mr Ping. She work for Mr Ping. When he see her, he like her. He buy her for his son. His son like to have the best girls – teach them, break them. He like her. She very pretty.'

'She's a child.'

He shrugs and his shoulders quiver. 'She fourteen. She very pretty. You like her? You like young girl? I get you girl like her. No problem. You win fight for –'

'Fuck it. Forget it. I don't want a girl.'

There's a long silence. He reaches out and puts a hand on my thigh with a leery smile. 'You want boy?'

I give him a look. 'No.'

'OK, OK. No boy. Have sleep. Fighting soon.'

He waddles to the door, his keys singing on his belt.

'Lee?' He turns, his eyebrows raised. 'Why does Ping cover his face when he talks to me?'

He looks at me and blinks. 'He little scared you maybe sick.'

'But why?'

'You English boy. England. America. Big disease. Everyone very sick. Dying.'

'What?'

'Yes. Big disease. Very bad. People very sick. Very scared.'

'Like an epidemic?' He doesn't understand the word. 'Er … outbreak? Virus? Bird Flu?'

He considers the question, picking at a scab. 'Virus. Yes,' he says slowly, 'not Bird Flu, I don't think – very, very bad. But you not sick, I think?'

'No. I'm not. I'm not sick,' and the words come slowly because my mind is melting, frying. I turn away and sit down on the floor with my head in my hands. Rubbing at my eye sockets. My father's words come back to me: 'Things aren't what they were, everything's changed …'

He knew. He knew all along. He kept me in the dark – no internet, no phones – because he knew if I knew, he'd never keep me there. I feel sick.

Lee shrugs again, goes out and I hear the dead sound of the bolt being shot outside and a key turned in the lock.

I sit for what feels like hours, staring at the wall until the bolt goes again and it's Lee. In his hand is a bottle of something. He pulls me up and sits me on the stool. He takes my feet in his hands and smacks at them hard over and over. He binds my hands with bandages and ties them. I can't think anymore. I can't take in what's happening. He's rubbing me with some kind of foul-smelling oil all over my back and shoulders. It burns and prickles my skin and it brings me back.

'What is this stuff?'

'Good for you. Put on these.'

He hands me a crumpled paper bag. Inside is a pair of shorts in a garish green and yellow. I do as I'm told and when I'm done, he beams at me. 'Good. Good. Ready to fight.'

He beckons to the door and we leave together. As soon as I'm in the corridor, I hear it. A low rumble of a hundred voices coming from the room with the cage.

Lee rubs his hands. 'Remember, use everything, but first thinking too. You believe you can win – you can win.'

'You're insane,' I say.

He opens the door and the voices rise to a pitch. There's drumming too. All eyes are on me. The room is rammed: men in suits, men in trainers and vests. All have wads of notes in their hands. The room smells of stale sweat and beer. I move through the crowd with my head down, following Lee. All the way, hands reach out and pinch and prod at me.

Up ahead, the Rooster's waiting. He stalks the cage, head high, arms waving – but it's all so fucking hollow – a pantomime. I see him again, punching the boy – hear it – and I'm in knots.

'Lee,' I whisper. 'I'm not doing this. It's insane. I'm not a fighter – I'll take my chance with Ping – I can't do this.'

Lee turns and looks at me, blinks, but he doesn't seem to hear me. We're at the front now, just under the cage. A man with a fringe of dark hair snatches at my skin and twists it in his fingers. I turn, wrench my arm away, and as I do, I see her.

Apart from the crowd, who are standing, a few chairs have been put out, and there, in the centre, is Mr Ping, holding a painted fan in one hand. To his right is a chubby, younger man wearing a fur coat. His black hair is glossed and piled up on his head. And in between them sits Yun. She's wearing a kind of silky dress buttoned up to the neck, and bright lipstick. She stares ahead of her into the middle distance, seemingly unaware of what's happening around her. I catch her eye and I try to smile but I know from what's probably happened to her, and what's about to happen to me, there isn't much for either of us to smile about.

The man in the fur coat drops a fleshy hand on her shoulder. He's wearing rings that catch in the strip lights. She flinches under him and the sight of it makes me so angry that when I get in the ring I'm ready to chew the Rooster up and spit him out. I shake out my limbs, set my eyes on him, and draw in my fists tight.

Rooster's like wood and wire. His skin glistens under the lights and I can smell the oil on him too. His hands are bandaged like mine and he dances in front of me, a smirk on his face, his feet barely touching the canvas floor. A bald man in a blue tracksuit steps into the ring, and the crowd is silent. I keep my eyes on

Yun. There's a streak of black on her cheek where her make-up has run.

The bald man is addressing the crowd. There are jeers and cheers as they jostle for a better view.

He turns to us and speaks to me in broken English: 'Rules: no rules. No breaks. When one down, other winner. Understand?'

I nod. He nods to Rooster, who kisses his fist, then he ducks out of the ring and the cage is locked and we're left to face each other.

Rooster's smaller than me and lighter. Which is good and bad. I'm probably stronger behind a punch but he's done this before and I've got to catch him first. He's weaving his way around the ring, keeping his distance. The crowd is roaring – angry and excited. I ape his dance, fists up, and look for a way in. But like the man said, there are no rules here, and, as I round the ring for a second time, he grabs me by the arm and pulls me under him. He aims a kick at my jaw with the sole of his foot and the crowd screams. I can taste warm metal now, blood under my tongue.

I roll and slam onto the floor and I find it – that black hole – sucking at me, pulling me in. I'm up and after him and I wrench him off his feet and send him flying. I kick him in the side and he doubles over. He's trying to get up when I slam him again against the side of the cage. He's bleeding now and I go after him with a sharp jab to his jawbone. Another under his ribs. He comes back then, slicing at me with his shins and elbows and they go home on my side where I was hurt before. But I grab his leg, twist, and with all my strength, I land him. The canvas floor puckers and shudders under him.

He's gone down head first but he shoots a kick at my ankles which knocks me off balance. I feel a shot of evil pain that runs up towards my hip. I can feel the muscles contracting inside me. Both on the floor now, we grapple, and he closes his mouth over my ear and bites. From the corner of my eye I see him pull away with what looks like half my ear lobe between his teeth.

When he's on his feet, he throws the piece of flesh out over the cage into the crowd. Blood's pouring down my neck and there's mist in front of my eyes. For a split second I catch Yun's face in the crowd. Pale and frightened. I ball into him, into the tight bands of muscle in his stomach, driving him against the wire, and as he hangs there winded for a moment, I bring back my fist and hook him in the ribs and he reels as the bone bites. He tries to come at me but I go in again ramming my fist into him with everything I've got. He staggers back, confused, and then falls against me.

And I don't even know how I do it but I bring him down and a punch to his head leaves him limp and twisted, blood pooling around him on the floor.

And again, I'm a million miles away. Spinning into blackness. And planet earth and all this, all of me, we're just specks of dust.

It all happens very quickly after that. The cage is unlocked and the bald man dips in. I'm walked round the ring for the crowd. They jostle to see me and I hear the crackle of bank notes changing hands. I stand in the centre listing this way and that. Rooster isn't moving. The ref gives him a sharp kick in the ribs and I'm relieved to hear him groan.

Bets settled, money won and lost, the crowd starts to go. As I step out of the cage, Mr Ping is there to meet me. He holds his fan against his face as he speaks.

'Good. Good. I was right. You are good fighter.' He grazes the skin on my arm with his sharp fingernails, and his touch makes me want to heave. The man in the furs stands behind him eyeing me carefully.

'My son,' says Mr Ping. He nods at me briefly and I stare. This is who Yun was bought for. Up close, he's a big guy. Soft pink fingers play over his mouth. Yun stands behind him and there's nothing I can do. When I turn back, Lee's there with Rooster hanging folded over his shoulder.

He pats me on the back. 'Good boy. Lee find you girl, yes?' He chuckles and Mr Ping nods. 'Yes. Nice girl for this boy. Nice girl to pleasure you tonight? You fight again for me soon.'

And I take the chance offered. I point at Yun. 'I want that girl.'

6

Her eyes widen. Mr Ping and his son look at me in disbelief. His son says something I don't understand, steps forward and smacks me hard across the face with the back of his hand. The force of it sends my teeth buzzing in my head. There's a frantic, whispered conversation between them and he produces a handkerchief and closes it over his mouth and steps back. Lee's pulling me away when Mr Ping says, 'That girl is mine. My son's. You have other girls. Pretty girls.' And here he talks to Lee who shifts Rooster onto his other shoulder as he listens.

'No. I want her. I'll fight for her. You say who I fight, and if I win, I take her.'

The son shrieks and comes for me again but Mr Ping snaps his fingers. The son turns and ushers Yun away. His hand's on her neck. She tries to turn but I can see he's squeezing her tight.

Ping's watching me, he smiles. 'That girl is my property ... like you. She's not for you. You good fighter,

I find good girl for you.' He waves at Lee who pulls and pushes me out into the corridor.

Lee sets down Rooster in his cell. I'm glad to see he's OK, and Lee reassures me he's had worse.

Lee comes and washes my cuts and bandages my ear. The cloths are clogged and soaked in my blood, and when he unties the bandages from my hands, my knuckles are swollen and misshapen: great dark blooms across every joint. He leaves me in the cell on the mattress and locks the door. I try to rest but I'm so jumpy, so wired. I've never felt like this before – like I'm high. I can still hear the crunch of my fist on his ribs, the smack of my foot on his face and Rooster lying on the floor bloodied and beaten.

And then it's gone. It's all gone. Like a gust of wind on a candle, the feeling goes, and I'm left with an empty bleak black that sinks into my bones – like rage, like suicide, like being buried alive.

I lie back on the mattress with my hands in my hair. Every movement hurts. I stretch out and look up at the thin window by the ceiling. Yun. I can't leave her here.

When I get out of here – because after what Lee told me, I know I have to get home as soon as possible – I have to find a way to help her. But I saw Ping's face when I talked about fighting for her. He'd liked it. Just for a moment he'd liked it. I was an idiot. It was too soon. He knows I want her. I've just given him something else to hold over me.

Just then the bolt's drawn on the outside and Lee's there. Grinning like a moron. He wipes his hands on his vest and steps aside. Behind him is a girl holding a tray of steaming bowls. She's beautiful – her skin glitters like gold dust and her eyes are dark with long lashes. At Lee's bidding, she smiles nervously and comes forward and then I realise with a start that she's for me. She's my reward.

'Nice girl from Mr Ping. Eat first!' he says with another earthy chuckle, and he leaves with a sort of bow like some bell boy in a smart hotel, closes the door and locks us in.

'Fuck,' is all I can muster right then. I stand up and she shrinks back slightly. The room feels smaller than ever. 'It's OK,' I say. 'I won't hurt you. I'm not going to … never mind. You speak English?'

She bows and offers the tray. I take it from her and put it on the floor. She clasps her hands and looks down. I'm so much bigger than her, I realise she's probably scared witless, and I sit back down again on the mattress and take up a bowl. 'You want some?' I say, keeping my voice soft.

She looks at me out of the corner of her eye. 'It's good. It's really good,' I say, with my mouth full of rice. I offer a bowl and she comes towards me. I shift down the mattress to make room but she kneels on the floor and then back on her haunches. She's wearing one of those dresses like Yun had on: like a silky tube, split from the hip and buttoned to the neck. She takes a bowl and begins to eat a little, picking out little curls of prawns and vegetables with her fingers.

After a while, she looks up and smiles at me. I stop eating and put my hands in my lap. Her gaze follows them and she puts down her bowl and takes my hand in hers. Her touch is so gentle it takes my breath away. She strokes my battered fingers from knuckle to tip and the cell is filled with the sound of our breathing. Her hair falls forward and brushes my forearm, and at once, the hairs on my arm prickle. It's so long since anyone touched me this way and even though I know she's been made to do it, that it's the last thing I even deserve, and that, like me, she's owned by Ping, it feels immense. Ridiculously fucking amazing.

I lie back on the mattress and she's still stroking my hand. And I let her fingers play up my bruised arms and onto my chest. She's leaning over me now, the ends of her hair just kissing my face. I close my eyes for a moment and take her arms and pull her towards me. And then I stop. And I sit up. Because what I'm doing, what I want to do, what I was thinking about doing, is so wrong in so many ways that it takes me a minute to get back inside myself and fully contemplate it.

'I'm sorry,' I say, shaking my head. She looks worried. Scared. 'It's not … I … you're lovely. But I don't want to do this. Not here. Not when we've been told this is what we've got to do. I don't want to feel like that. And … and …' and I say this knowing full well that the idea that Sophy's been faithful to me for the best part of a year is pretty ridiculous. 'I have a girlfriend.' I'm right. It even sounds ridiculous. Like here and now, after everything that's happened, why on earth does that matter? Where does that even fit in? Except that it does. It means everything.

'It's OK,' she smiles. 'You are scared. I am scared.'

'No! I'm not. I mean I'm not scared enough to do this to you. With you. Do you understand?'

She nods slowly.

'What's your name? I'm Ben.'

She coughs and whispers it: 'Kamala.'

'Kamala.'

'Yes.'

'Let's eat, Kamala.'

And as we eat, I watch her and she watches me and I wonder if …

'Hey, do you know a girl called Yun? She ran away. Came back yesterday?'

'Yun? With blue eyes?'

'Yeah. Do you know her?'

'She with Mr Bao Zhi?'

'Er … Mr Ping's son? Yes.'

For a long time, she looks at me, a little handful of beansprouts held aloft on their way to her mouth.

'I want to help her,' I say, by way of explanation.

She nods slowly and says, 'She live with Mr Ping. In Mr Ping house. With Bao Zhi.'

'Where do you live?'

'In town. I live with other girls.'

She doesn't need to say anymore. 'Where are you from?'

'From Thailand.'

'Your parents?'

'Mother dead. My father ill can't work. Mr Ping pay for me. I work for him. He look after my father. I work –'

'And there are other girls there? How many?'

She holds up the fingers on both hands.

'Ten? Ten girls?'

She nods.

'And was Yun there?'

'Yun very special. When Mr Ping see her, he want her for Bao Zhi. He send men to come to take her. She very scared so she run away.'

'And he sent his men after her.'

'He pay lot of money for us. We run away, he find us and beat us. He always find us. Always.'

'So you have to work. To … to do this?'

She nods, and after a minute she begins to stroke my chest, trailing her hand to my waist. I stop her. 'You don't have to do this with me. You don't have to do this. I don't want you to.'

'He beat me if I don't please you.'

'Listen. Stop. It's OK. I'll tell him you pleased me. It's OK. You can trust me. You can. I promise. But I need you to help me too.'

She looks up.

'Can you get to a phone? You have a phone where you are?'

Her eyes widen and she looks around her before nodding once.

'I need to get a message to someone – In England. In the U.K. I want you to tell them I'm alive – that I'm OK. Can you do that?'

She smiles. 'I will try.'

'If you can. If it's possible, yeah? Don't get in trouble.'

'What is the number?'

I look around and she follows my gaze. In the corner, there's a little pile of sandy stones about the size of my palm. I grab one, and the other I chip against the wall until it's a point. It takes a while but eventually the larger stone holds two numbers: Charlie's and Sophy's.

'Just tell them I'm alive. If you can.' ·

She takes the stone and runs her hand over it. She nods once. 'I will try for you, Ben.'

'Thank you. Thank you.'

She leans her head against my chest for a moment and I catch her. The smell of her hair takes me straight to Sophy and I hold her. We stay like this while the world spins around us until the door outside is unlocked and Lee comes in with a wide grin. 'Good time for you? Yes? Good time with girl?'

I nod enthusiastically. 'Very good. Yeah. Good.'

She stands back with her head bowed. I see the line of the stone in the pocket of her dress. Lee says something to her and she gives me a dip of the head and steps outside. He winks at me and I return his grin, feeling sick to my stomach.

7

I lie awake for hours, staring at the ceiling. Apart from the odd grunt or howl, it's quiet. My muscles are slowly starting to unwind. There's a fat wad of dressing over my ear and it hurts like fuck.

I can still smell Kamala in the room. Still feel her fingertips on my skin.

I turn into the wall and I think about home: about Mum before she died, about Maurice; and then my Dad. His hands: on me, on that steering wheel. His eyes. And then the things he did and didn't do. This sickness. This virus in the West that Lee talked about: it spins and sparks and crashes in my head. Could this be something to do with him – with Rees?

If it is down to them, if this epidemic is a part of what he did there, then it's down to me too. He made me a part of it – made me the cure. It's in me. And what he did to me, what he made me, means I'm worth a lot back home … means whatever I do, I have to get out of here.

That picture haunts me – the engraving from my father's wall. The dark woods. I'm back there again in his study with that faint smell of furniture polish, and him bent over his papers, working. Then I turn over, curl into myself, and he's in my head as I sleep.

Lee wakes me in the morning and I follow him to the wash room: concrete floor, cracked tiles on the walls, and a single toilet stall. There's a line of basins, and at the end, three shower heads. I see Rooster there, his body bent under the spray. His skin is greenish under the strip lights and covered in bruises, some old, some new. I swallow hard. Lee shoves a rough towel at me and pushes me towards the showers. Rooster looks round as I approach, and nods. I undress, eyeing him warily, and he hands me a sliver of soap. His knuckles are raw.

'You OK?' I ask under my breath.

He looks at me sharp and nods. 'You?'

'Yeah.'

He's drying himself now and I duck under the shower and turn on the water. At once it's scalding on my skin, and then lukewarm. Another boy comes into the room and begins to shave at the sink. I've seen him before: a short, stocky guy with a baby face. He says something to Rooster and he grins at me. I finish up and grab at the towel. They stare at me. I can still hear Lee but he's outside.

'You fight good,' says Rooster. He's watching me sideways on through dark narrow eyes.

'I was lucky.'

'Ping likes you,' he says. The other boy's standing near him now. I pull on my clothes, still feeling the sting of soap and water on my skin.

I shrug. I listen for Lee but he's gone. Baby Face steps towards me, and at once I'm tense. But Rooster just leans back against a sink. There's a livid open cut on his cheek from our fight. I finger my bad ear.

'Who cut your teeth that way?' I ask. He grins and runs his tongue over them. Up close the points are rough and uneven.

'Ping.'

'Jesus,' I breathe. He shrugs. I say, 'How long have you been here?' In answer he holds up a hand and opens four crooked fingers.

'Four years? How come?'

He rubs his thumb and forefinger together. 'Money.'

'Like Kamala.'

He stands up at the mention of her name. 'You know Kamala?' I nod. He's up in my face now, breathing hard. 'How? How do you know her?'

I return his look and he smacks at the wall next to me with the flat of his hand. 'When?'

'Last night,' I say, and then because I see the look on his face, quickly: 'nothing happened.'

His hand's on my throat now and the sharp nails cut at my flesh. 'You fuck her? You fuck her?'

'No. Ping sent her! I didn't want … I didn't. She came and stayed but I didn't … I have a girlfr –' and

I tail off then because it sounds so fucking lame. He releases his grip and says something to Baby Face who grunts and scratches his balls.

'OK.'

'You like Kamala? She's your … girlfriend?' I ask. He looks at me for a long time and it's all quiet except for a tap dripping onto concrete and the dogs barking.

'I like her.'

Baby Face slaps him on the back and shakes his head. I say, 'She's nice.'

He spits on the floor at my feet. 'You don't touch her.'

'Look, I didn't ask for her. Ping sent –'

He spits again at the mention of the name and the froth of the spit spirals in the drain water under the sink and disappears.

'I'm sorry,' I say. 'I'd feel the same if it was me – my girl – I …' But it's all just noise because right now no one has a say in any of this, and anyway, I was going to say that I'd never touch her, do anything with her but way, way, way in the back of my mind maybe, just maybe, I'm not sure I really mean that. And not only does that make me an A1 prick, it also makes me a total coward because I know if he knew for a moment what had gone through my mind when I was with her, he'd pull my head off and crap in it.

I change the subject. 'Haven't you ever tried to get out of here?'

They both look up. And after a minute or two when I think that maybe he's going to kill me after all,

Rooster comes up close again. He pulls up his shirt and turns. Across his back and side are four deep silvered welts each about 6 inches long. The skin around them is puckered and tight.

It's Baby Face who says it: 'No good.'

'Shit,' I'm choking. Suddenly all the air is pulled out of the room. 'Ping did this?'

He nods. 'I try to get out after I come here. I was fifteen. He catch me and he burn me. If I try again, he will kill me.'

'How did you come to be here?'

'Taken. Like you. I know my family try to find me – but they scared – Ping very … very powerful man.'

I whisper, 'But if you did it, if you could get out, if you had help … where would you go?' For a single moment, his eyes widen and I see something else there: hope maybe. He shrugs, and then it's like he's made up his mind. He crosses to the door and checks down the passage. Baby Face picks his nose and looks me up and down, his stomach straining against his vest.

Rooster comes back then and he says to me, 'Why?'

'Because … because – *what the fuck* – I'm not staying here – I have to get out. There has to be a way out.'

He shakes his head. 'At first, everyone thinks that.'

I fold my arms. Baby Face is staring at me – he looks interested. 'All I'm asking is, do you have somewhere – someone – you could go to? If you did get out?'

He shrugs, looks behind him, then at Baby Face, and a look passes between them. 'Maybe,' he says.

The dripping's stopped but I hear fat footsteps on the floor. Lee's coming back.

I stare at him, he looks at me, and the intensity in that look is crazy. I'm about to say something, anything, when I see Lee come into the room with two other boys, one bloodied, with his arm in a makeshift sling. Rooster shakes his head and turns to the sink.

Lee's gives Baby Face a friendly pat on the arse, and Rooster dips his head under the tap.

Lee says to me, 'You lucky boy. Have nice time with girl last night, now Mr Ping want to talk you about a big fight.'

Rooster's hair stands up in wet spikes and his eyes are cold. He pushes past us and I hear his steps fall away. Baby Face trots after him. Lee pushes the others towards the showers and pulls me by the arm. 'Come come. Mr Ping waiting.'

There are two people in my cell: Ping's there, and as I come in, he whisks a handkerchief over his nose. He seems nervous. The other guy is tall and thin with a pointed chin and eyebrows that meet in the middle. Diamonds wink on his cuffs, and he also carries a heavily scented handkerchief. The perfume fills the room and settles on everything like pollen.

'This is Mr Chai. He is from Thailand.'

The thin man inclines his head ever so slightly. I look from one to the other. Ping says something to Lee who disappears and returns, puffing, with a couple of chairs. They sit and I stand. My hands are balled against my sides. I can feel the blood knocking at my wrists.

Ping says, 'Off shirt.' I pull off my shirt and stand staring at the wall behind them. Ping points approvingly, still holding the handkerchief.

Mr Chai creaks forward in his chair. 'This is the boy? This boy? This is the best you can come up with? This boy isn't a fighter. My boy's a professional. Champion of the cages.' He speaks with a squeaky American accent. I hear Lee breathe out behind me. Mr Chai turns back to Ping. 'Waste of time.' He waits with his mouth half open and his lower lip hanging like a fish.

There's a long pause and I see Ping's left eyelid twitch. After a while he leans back, snaps his fingers and speaks to Lee, who looks at him a long time, then leaves the room. Mr Chai smiles at Ping and I'm just putting my shirt back on when there's a scuffle at the cell door. Lee's standing wide eyed in the doorway, holding a boy loosely by the arm: Baby Face.

His head's hanging but his body's taut. He looks chubby but when I clock him, close up, under the skin, he's solid, really built: thick neck and wide shoulders. His hands are closed against his sides and there's bright green tattoo ink on every knuckle. Mr Ping claps his hands. We're all squeezed in this tiny cell and the strip light whines and the perfume's making me want to retch when Ping gets up, goes outside, and motions to Mr Chai to do the same. Lee follows them with the chairs, and we're left facing each other.

Ping comes back in and says to me, really casual like he's asking me the time, 'Kill him.'

Lee shuffles and shakes his head. Baby Face looks at him and me and we both look at Ping.

I say, 'No.'

Chai looks up.

Ping says, 'Yes.' I stare at him, defiant and he lowers his handkerchief and leans up and speaks into my ear: 'You know what is the purse for this fight – you and Mr Chai's boy?' I pull back and look at him. 'Prize? Will be a ... a private game: me and Mr Chai.' He hisses the words: 'You know what Mr Chai want if his boy win?' A sick feeling creeps up into my throat. He knows I know. He nods. 'Yes ... is girl. Little Yun. Mr Chai like her. He want to take her back to Thailand. High class work. American clients.'

Mr Chai smiles and nods.

Lee's there to stop me before I land a punch on Ping's face. Ping scuttles back behind the bars, Lee shoves me back against the wall and Baby Face doesn't wait to be told. He slams into me with his whole body, and for a moment I'm winded like a beached fish. He lands a kick in my side with the flat of his foot, and something in me switches. I grab his ankle and twist. He yelps and grabs at the air. I'm on my feet then and I rack up a couple of good punches that throw him away from me. It gives me a second to think and I go for the belly. Feet first. He gags at the first blow then throws up with the second and he's getting to his feet but swaying when I whack him in the head with my elbow which floors him again.

I watch him slap on the floor at my feet. The flesh on him ripples and shudders. He paws at the ground and is quiet, there's vomit on his hands. And suddenly it rushes at me and I can't move for what I'm feeling. I can't speak or hear or see. I slump down on the mattress and I put my head in my hands and all I can see is blood.

8

There's a clang as the door is opened and the low murmur of voices. I open my eyes.

Lee's crouching over Baby Face. He's lost it. There's a weird look in his eyes like he's angry and sad and disappointed and lost and head-fucked all at the same time. And ashamed. Yeah, he looks kind of ashamed. He leans over Baby Face with a towel and dabs at his nose and mouth. He looks at me and his eyes are wet. I can't look at him. Chai comes in, stepping over Baby Face to get to me. In the background, Ping catches my eye and nods.

Chai says, 'You're sharper than you look. Needs training, but he's feisty. Yeah ... there's something about him. Hungry ... Next week I'll bring my boy over. We'll have some fun.'

There's a cry from Baby Face and I go to him. His breath comes in faint wheezes. Ping stands over him. He pushes at him with a polished toe and turns to me. 'I told you to kill him.'

I face him. 'No.'

His nostrils flare, and for a second I think I see something that looks almost like fear flash across his face. Lee looks up at me and Baby Face groans. Ping waits and I think he's trying to decide what to say or do and in the end he says, 'Next time. Training now.' He barks something at Lee and leaves the cell.

I squat down with Lee who's cradling Baby Face's head in his lap. 'Will he be OK?'

Lee manages a smile. 'I hope. I hope so, Ben.'

I nod. Together we manage to half-lift, half-walk him back to his cell. When we get in there, there are pictures on the walls torn out of magazines. Weird pictures. Gaudy, bright-coloured advertisement spreads for washing powder and cars and lipstick. And there's something so pathetic, so fucking hopeful and hopeless about it that I feel myself choking,

I turn to Lee, careful to lower my voice. 'What are you doing here, Lee? This is shit – this life. Why do you do it? Why don't you get out?'

He's settling Baby Face onto his mattress and he turns to me with a kind of smile and a shrug that reminds me of Rooster, and says, 'You work for Mr Ping, you never get out.'

'How long have you –?'

He cuts me off. 'I was ten years old, no mother, father – living on the streets – Mr Ping take me, train me.' He shrugs again and I can feel that black hopelessness pooling around me like treacle and I know I have to get away from here before it pushes up and sinks me.

'You could – they could –' I know I'm taking a big risk here but there was something in the way he looked at Baby Face that makes me do it anyway.

He raises an eyebrow. I go on: 'Listen,' I say. 'I'm not staying in here – I've wasted enough of my life. I'm going to get out. I don't how yet but …' I look at Baby Face who seems to be half listening, drifting in and out of consciousness, and realise then I don't even know his real name. 'Will you help me? You've got the keys, you could –'

Lee breaks away from Baby Face and looks at me as he scratches and picks at the scabs on his head. 'No no no, Mr Ping very powerful man. You don't understand. He will –'

'Yeah, yeah, I know. I know what – I heard all that. But I'm not going to spend the rest of my life in this place.' I don't say, "like you" but I guess right then I don't need to. 'Think about it.'

There's a wait and he shakes his head and coughs a bit and turns back to Baby Face and I'm no clearer. I go out to the exercise yard where I see Rooster; he's leaning by the fence smoking. He offers me a skinny roll-up.

'I'm sorry. About your friend.'

He shrugs. 'Normal.'

'I didn't have a choice.'

He stares at me. 'Choice?'

And then I feel like an idiot because the whole idea of having a choice about anything ever is probably so totally alien to him that it's ridiculous, and yet, I guess if I think about it, I did have a choice – except that it was the same as before – the only choice here is either kill or be killed and I've already proved to myself how much I want to go on living. He offers me a smoke and I take it. Standing there, pulling smoke into my lungs, feeling the burn low in my throat, I feel better. I look out at the buildings over the fence. Tall weeds and graffiti and the red haze in the sky over the city.

I hesitate, then I come out with it. 'Hey, I wanted to talk to you … what we were saying this morning. You said you knew somewhere … safe, maybe? Somewhere you could go?'

His black eyes flicker and he pinches a curl of tobacco from his tongue. 'Forget it.'

'Forget it? That's it?' I say. 'You're OK with all this? Fuck that.' I go to move away, feeling the rub of the fence up and down my arm.

He follows me. 'I think about it – everyone thinks about it,' he says, 'but you don't know Ping.'

'What's there to know? It's not complicated – he's a psycho – I knew that the minute I laid eyes on him.'

He folds his arms. 'You can't win. You will not win.'

I look at him, pull on my cigarette. 'Yeah, well I'm going to try anyway. I asked Lee about it.'

'You told Lee? Why?'

'Because I trust him, because I think he's had enough.'

'You are here a few days and you know that?' he says. 'You're crazy. You don't know how it feels to have enough.'

'Yeah. As it happens, I do. I do know.'

He crushes his cigarette tip into his palm. He doesn't even flinch. 'Only way you ever get out is you kill him.'

9

Sophy

It's bad. I know it's bad. She's trying to hide it but I can see the pin-head blisters blooming on the back of her neck like little mushrooms. Soon they'll have spread to her face; soon her eyes and nose will be bleeding. She lies on the couch and waits, and all I can do is wait too, feeling my breath steam and bubble in the mask.

We're all waiting. Dad's hung a bed sheet from the top front window. It catches the breeze and claps against the side of the house like a giant wing. Everyone who sees will know what it means; we've all had it hammered in to us:

In the event of an infection call the above number and display a white flag or sheet that can be clearly seen from the street. Wait for assistance from the Bio Team. Do NOT under any circumstances leave the house. Failure to comply with the above will be treated as a criminal act.

Last week, a man in London whose wife was sick, went crazy. He ran out of the house and up the street, and they shot him. Killed him like a dog. Everyone knows about the snipers. They sit in parked cars, on rooftops. They'll be in place already, waiting for a twitch in the curtains or the turn of a door handle on an infected house. Just like everyone will know about us: about how we've lost. What's happened means we're no longer in the big boat, the same boat, we're no longer part of the 'survivors': we've cut ourselves away, on a raft in open water. Cut away from everything and everyone. And there'll be no one leaning over the side to wave us off. No one will want to know. Because this is how it works: one person will infect at least three people; their breath, skin, even their hair, are infectious. It's hopeless.

Ten minutes later, they're ringing the bell. Mum's eyes over the white of her mask are blanks and Dad shows them in. They're head to foot in rubberized bio gear: big oxygen tanks on their backs, and goggles, gloves, suits, the lot. Their voices are distorted through their helmets and their suits rustle and crunch as they move. I think, I never thought this would happen to us, never thought that somehow we'd be the family it came to. I try to find Ben but he's gone. His face, his touch, and the news that had lifted me in the morning, are all gone. I cannot get him back. All of me, my flesh and my bones are all with my sister.

By the time they come for her, sweat is beading on her swollen face and her eyes are shot. She cries when they lift her. They carry her out of the room in a kind of polythene cage. And they're talking to her but she's shaking her head and then she's screaming and I'm trying to calm her down and when I look at Mum, she's standing in the corner of the room just staring, like she's watching it on a film or a news report, like she's not even there and it drives me mad.

'Mum! Hey, Mum! Aren't you going to comfort her? Your daughter? She's scared witless, can't you see? MUM!!' and everyone turns at that – the guys in the orange suits – then Dad comes in with an armful of coats and shouts back: 'Leave your mother alone! This is probably you! Down to you this – I expect. Going out all the time when I expressly told you not to!'

One of the men in the suits turns to me. 'What's that about? You been out? Where?'

I can't see his face through his helmet and I don't give a fuck anyway. All I care about is Lily. 'Yes. I've been out. Before I knew she was sick. It's not against the law.'

'Mmm,' he breathes. 'You speak to anyone? Touch any animals?'

'Er … Yes, and No.'

Dad's screaming now. His Adam's apple's snapping up and down. 'What does that mean? What the hell does that mean? Just answer the question can you? This is serious!'

'Oh really? Is it? What exactly is serious, Dad? Me going out or my sister dying?' And as soon as the word's out of my mouth I feel sick for having said it because I can see the top of her head under the cage and it jerks sharply and she's crying again, and I've just made things ten million times worse. The guy helps. A bit. He says gently, like it's a dig at Dad to shut up and calm the fuck down: 'You spoke to someone?'

I nod slowly and the room is quiet. The others are struggling down the narrow hall with Lily, brushing at pictures and sending ornaments flying. I see Mum look up as a china bulldog hits the floor and shatters.

'He was masked.'

'Who? Name? Address?'

'Josh James. He's a ... he was in my class ... he's a soldier. He was on the roadblock here at the end.'

Dad's up again. 'Chatting up soldiers is it? Lovely. Just lovely.' He looks around for back-up but Mum's gone.

The guy nods. 'Thank you. And that's it? No one else?'

I shake my head and glare at Dad.

The guy hands us masks and gloves and turns. 'Right, Follow me.' Dad and I stare after him for a moment and he turns and says, 'You'll all need to be tested and quarantined.'

Mum says, 'Can we pack a bag?'

'Sorry. You won't be able to keep anything once we're there. Let's get your sister in.'

And we follow him, and every curtain, in every house is tweaked and twitched as we leave, and the white sheet rises and falls like a sail as Dad closes the door behind us.

At the hospital, we're moved into the Isolation Unit at top speed, and before I really have a chance to know what's going on, I find myself in a locked room on a closed ward in a hospital gown and a mask. There's a window onto the street and one onto the ward, and from time to time, masked medical people come and look at me through it like I'm some kind of exhibit. Until I get the hang of the blinds, that is.

There's a bed and a chair and a cabinet and a small toilet and shower cubicle. I lie on the bed and I don't move. It's like everything's gone, it's all been sucked out of me. All I can do is lie here watching my chest fall and rise and fall again, see my breath as it leaves me, pucker and lift the thin gown. And I think how I'm empty, and how long it's been that I've felt this way.

There's a knock at the door, a total joke because it's not like they're not coming in. They've got the key after all. A little woman with a sloping shoulder comes in and sits in the chair a little way off from the bed. She's dressed in full bio gear.

'Hi,' she says brightly through the visor. She has a northern accent and a weird kind of speech impediment that sounds like she's trying to swallow her teeth. 'You OK? Can I get you anything?'

I shake my head. 'How's Lily?' And she doesn't answer me. She doesn't say anything, just fixes me with watery eyes. I say, '*What*?' and she shakes her head. I say it again: '*What*? Is she OK?'

Silence, and I'm crying, choking tears through this stupid mask. My nose is running.

She looks at my panic like she's far away, and says, 'I can't say anything at this stage, Sophy. We don't know.'

'I thought –'

'I know. I'm sorry.' She gets up then and moves to the window and opens the blinds and I realise it's not her shoulder that's crooked it's her back. Her spine curves out like a bicycle wheel. She waves at a nurse who nods and sprints off.

'We need to start doing some tests, OK?' I nod. She pulls a small notebook from her pocket. 'The team will be here in a minute. I just want to ask you a few questions. Did your sister go out at all in the last few days? Mix with anyone outside of the family?'

'No. No. Mum wouldn't let her …'

'Animals?'

'No.'

'And you, how are you feeling? Any temperature?'

I shake my head. I say, 'I heard there'd been a case of it in town?'

She looks up from her notes. 'Where did you hear that?'

'Has there?'

She breathes out quietly, steaming the visor. And the world stops. I hear voices, look up at the window and I see Josh being brought in. He passes the window but his eyes are blank. She follows my gaze. 'You know him?'

I nod slowly. 'Josh. The guy I spoke to. Why is he in here?'

'Tests. Anyone you or your family's been in contact with needs to come in. That's why we need to make absolutely sure there's no one else. You see?'

I nod again. 'There's no one ... listen, can I get a phone in here?'

She raises her eyebrows.

'I just need ... a friend ... I just said I'd call –'

'Who's that? Someone we should –'

'No. I haven't seen him for months. I just want to ... I had some news.' I catch the look in her eyes. 'It's nothing to do with this, I promise. Please?'

'You'll have to be quick. The team's finishing up with your Mum and Dad. There's a phone here. Press 411 to get an outside line.'

'Thanks.'

Left on my own again, I pull the mask off and rub my hands against my face, through my hair. There's something weirdly comforting about it, like the press and smell of someone else's skin on mine. I straighten up and get the phone. It's ages before he answers, and when he does, I can hardly hear him.

'Charlie?'

'Sophy. Hey. What's up? You OK?'

'I'm ... no. I'm in hospital. Quarantine.'

I hear him breathe out. 'Shit.'

'It's Lily ...' I will myself not to cry.

'Ah, Soph, I'm so ... I'm ... shit. I don't know what to say ... is it definite?'

'Thanks. I don't know. I mean, they don't know.'

I'm fighting tears but I have to get to it. 'Listen, Charlie, I have to tell you something ...' A sharp rap on the door stops me in my tracks and a guy in the orange bio gear makes like he's about to come in. I shout. 'WAIT! Please? Please? Just give me a minute?'

The guy hesitates then nods and backs out, and I'm back with Charlie.

'What? What is it?'

'It's Ben. I heard something. He's alive.'

A silence. 'No way. You're kidding. You ... must ... How ...? I mean, how −?'

'I had a call. From someone. A girl. In ... in China.'

'China? *He's still there?* Then what the fuck's he been doing all this time? I mean what could have stopped him from −?'

'I don't know but I ... if I get out of this I really want to help him. And if I don't ... then I want you ... I wanted you to know.'

'Where is he?'

'I don't know. I don't know. She didn't say. Can I call you again? I have to have these tests and stuff.'

'Christ, yes. God, Soph I can't take it in ...'

'I know ... I −'

'Listen,' he says, whispering now: 'they'll shoot me if they find out I told you this but I want you to know. I heard something the other day.' There's another knock on the door. I ignore it.

'What?'

'About this − all this − this virus.'

'Charlie, *what?*'

There's a pause on the line and I can hear the wires whisper. 'You can't tell a soul, Soph. You've got to promise. They'll end me if they know.'

I swallow. 'I promise. Just tell me.'

'OK. It isn't just another epidemic – bird flu or something, like they're saying. It's a … it's terrorism. This virus is weaponised. Germ warfare – that's what we're dealing with. Bio-warfare. And you know what else?'

I say nothing but my fingers are blue, twisted in the phone flex.

'Well, it's a neo-Marxist group with links to the North Koreans. They're based – at least, we think they're based – in China.'

'Shit.'

'I know. They say they want a reunited Korea. And all kinds of crazy demands. They're waiting till we fall apart then … I guess … well … they'll have the vaccine. When they get what they want they'll hand it over. Governments in the west have been trying to keep it secret up to now – news on lockdown – internet, everything, but –'

A coldness creeps under my skin. I don't know what I say, what I do next. Before I know what's going on, the phone's back in its cradle and someone's pushing a needle into my arm. I think I must have dropped the phone when I heard it. I lie on the bed and watch the dark blood pulsing into a tube. My blood. And I'm thinking – what Charlie said – does any of it have to do with Ben? With his dad?

I try to focus. I ask, 'When will you know? About my sister?'

One of them shakes his head. 'Soon. You too.' He packs up and without looking at me says, 'Try and get some rest.'

'The guy you brought in,' I say, 'the soldier? Where is he?'

The two of them look at each other and one answers, 'Next room. Good night.'

They lock the door again when they leave. I close the blinds, turn down the light and sit on the bed. They've taken my clothes. Suddenly I'm very cold. I peel a thin blanket off the bed and wrap it about my shoulders. I still have the phone and I think about phoning Charlie back but I can't talk to him right now.

David Collins. A virus to end all viruses. China. And Ben? What had happened to Ben? He'd talked about … what was it …? Finishing his dead father's work? Helping him … *closure*? Something like that. Has he been a part of this? Been a part of what was happening to me? To Lily? Would he, could he? And his face comes back to me, and his hands are on my body, and he's so gentle, so loving. I can't believe it. I don't want to believe it but then I really, truly don't know what to believe anymore.

It's nearly midnight when I hear a soft tapping on the wall by the bed. I wait and it stops and then I tap back. Two short knocks and then: 'Sophy?'

'Josh?'

'Hey.' His voice is surprisingly clear. I guess for all their locked doors the walls are paper thin. 'They said you were here.'

'Are you OK?' We both say it at once, and I let myself smile for a moment. And then I tell him about why we're here. Why he's here. He knows anyway.

'You know, it might not be what you think it is,' he says.

'I just want her to be alright.'

'And ... if it is ... some people do get better.'

'Really?'

'Yeah. I've heard of a few cases.'

'Oh.'

'I mean ... you know ... it's ...'

'Little girls?'

'Eh?'

'These people who've survived it, were any of them 8-year old girls?'

There' s a silence and I can hear him picking at the wall on the other side. 'I don't know. But they're getting to know this thing ... it won't be long before we've found a cure ...'

I swallow tears.

'Sophy ... You OK? You've gone quiet.'

I breathe. 'I'm OK. Just a bit preoccupied.'

'Of course. Listen, I'm sure she'll be OK. I wish I could give you a hug.'

And the thought of it makes me want to cry because right then, that's exactly what I want too. I go for a dry laugh. 'We've only seen each other twice and both times I've been a wreck.'

'Did you hear any more about Ben?'

'No. No I didn't. Nothing.'

'Oh.' He waits. 'I meant it about the hug you know.'

'I know. Thank you.'

'Don't thank me. It's not a present. Not cos I feel … sorry for you or anything, which I do. I mean, this is shit for you of course, but when I say, I'd like to … I mean, I like you, Sophy. Oh fuck. Way to mess up a line.'

'I didn't mean it like that. I meant, thank you, because I know you mean it. If that makes any sense. You've been really sweet, and I'm just sorry you had to be … involved.'

'No problem – I wish I could help – do something.'

We laugh. A bit. And then he says, 'I'm probably keeping you up. Get some sleep. I'm sure you'll have better news in the morning.'

'Thanks. Good night.'

'Good night.'

I hear him padding away from the wall and I call to him, 'Josh?'

'Yeah?'

'Did you ever hear anything about the virus, about why it started, where it came from?'

'What d'you mean? What? Like bird flu?'

'Yeah, or something else … I don't know.'

'No. Nothing. Why?'

'Oh nothing. I just wondered. Night.'

'Night night.'

I spend a long time after that looking out of the window onto the street, feeling fairly sure that he's doing the same in his room but I don't say anything. The street lights buzz and flicker and light up the piles of rubbish stacked on the pavements. There are rats fishing in and out of the bags, their pink tails like whips.

I go to sleep after that and I dream of crossing the sea and of Ben there waiting on the shore for me.

10

Rooster and Baby Face must have done some damage because I sleep badly, turning and stretching all night. There are sharp pains in my side and my ear feels hot and puffy and irritated.

The next day, there's no time to think about anything because I'm woken up early and put to work in the training ring. Lee's evasive – blank – he won't talk about what I said last night and it makes me think I was an idiot to ask him. I can't get him to talk about Baby Face either but when I passed it this morning, his cell was empty.

He shoves a length of wet rope at me and motions to me to skip. As I do, I'm thinking about what Rooster said about Ping. About killing him. Ping dead would change everything.

Every time I mess up, Lee takes a swipe at me. Every time I miss a beat, he's on me with his bamboo cane, smacking at my legs till my shins are burning. It's hot in the room and my neck and back are wet with sweat. And every time I slow up, he's on it. But I don't stop. And not because he's ready to pile into me if I do, but because I want this as much as he does, as much as Ping does. Because if I'm going to stand a chance of getting out of here, then I have to work at it. All the work outs I did in the camp – the press ups, pull ups – they just made me bulky, not fit. This is different. My arms and legs are boiling.

I must have slowed again because a whack on my shins makes me gasp and I drop the rope. There's another sound from behind me – a door opening and shutting. I look back and see Kamala watching me with wide eyes. She's standing by the wall, her palms flat against it, her fingernails showing blood red against the concrete. Lee notices her and pads over to the edge of the ring. I wait and watch, pulling in air as they talk.

She's wearing a skirt and a T-shirt, and her hair is pulled back off her face. I think about Rooster and the look on his face when I said she'd been in my cell with me, and I don't like it but I'm watching her all the same – her soft breasts under the T shirt, the curve of her neck where her hair's tied. The way her skin shines. And the smell of her: even from here, it's sweet like fruit, like I can taste it.

I'm lost in it when Lee comes over. 'Mr Ping send for you. He want to see you. You go with Kamala. Go get ready.'

I come back. 'Why?' I say. 'What for?'

'No time. Just go.'

Lee pats me on the back and calls to Kamala. I follow them down the stairs into my cell. I'm standing in the middle of the room with Lee, listening to the lights buzz and hum and the cockroaches tapping in the walls, when Kamala comes back with a bucket and a cloth. Slowly, carefully, she dips the cloth in the bucket and squeezes it, releasing fat splashes of water. With the cloth in her fist, she reaches up and pushes it gently against my face. I look down at her and her eyes are on me and then all down my chest there are streams of water crawling.

The water's warm, and the touch of it and her on my skin makes me shiver. She doesn't stop but strokes it across my shoulders and down the length of my arms, my hands and on the bruises on my fingers. She doesn't speak but her breath is sweet, and right at that moment I want her so much it scares me.

Lee says, 'Hurry hurry,' and goes out. I hear him trotting off down the corridor.

Then I take the cloth from her, drop it, and I take hold of her wet hands, turn them over in mine and they lie there curled upwards in mine. She looks up at me and her eyes are soft and bright. And I'm looking at the push and pout of her lips and I know I shouldn't be but I'm thinking about kissing her, when she says, 'The girl ...'

'What?'

'The girl. The telephone number you gave −'

Sophy. I'd almost forgotten her. I wake up. 'What? What did she say? Did you speak to her?'

She nods slowly. Her hands are still resting in mine, her breath coming and going on my chest. 'I told her you're alive.'

'And?'

'She ask if you are sick.'

'Is she … is she sick?'

She looks at me, shakes her head. 'I don't know. I had to go. I tell her you're alive – that you're in China. That's all.'

I drop her hands, go to the door and breathe. Before I know it, she's behind me, her hand on the small of my back. I turn and bend and hold her and she's breathing fast against me like a bird. I just hold her because she's the only thing in this place that makes me feel remotely human, and the more I think about that, the more miserable I feel about Sophy. But I console myself with one thought: at least she knows I'm alive.

I pull back. 'The other number?'

'No time.'

'OK. Of course. Thanks. Thanks, Kamala.'

I can hear Lee wheezing along the passage. He stops at the door, looks in at me and I follow his gaze. My face is wet and my body's covered in rusty streaks of blood like some weird war paint. He pads over to the bucket and upends it over me while Kamala watches.

'You are late, Ben. Ping waiting. Car outside.'

He says something to her and she nods and leaves with a last look at me. I'm pushing water off my face and when I look up, he's standing, and there's a weird look in his eyes. He leans forward and whispers, 'What you said. Before about getting out –'

'Yeah?'

There are footsteps outside and he whisks his head from side to side making his jowls wobble and shiver. 'Not now. You go. Time to go. Talk later.'

A couple of rampant stone dragons mark the entrance to Ping's house. And they're kind of the best bit because once we're inside the compound, it's grim: crunchy tarmac drive and a long grey bungalow with narrow windows.

Inside, it's all a kind of dog-brown on the walls and ceilings, with thick patterned rugs across hard floors. I'm shown in to what looks like his office. He's sitting at a marble-topped desk and he swings on his chair to face me. The wall behind him is hung with a set of elaborate daggers with green handles carved into animal heads.

He sees me looking. 'Jade. Antique. Very valuable.' I look at the floor. 'Training is good? Getting strong?'

I look at him, see his eyes flash over my body with something like greed or jealousy, I can't tell. He nods and sits back. 'When I saw you, *first time*, I knew. I knew you were good for me. You are ... angry – very angry. You want to fight but you have to believe in what you are fighting for. You think you are fighting to get out. To go home to your girl in England – I know. But I tell you Ben,' and he leans forward and fixes me with his eyes, 'you will never leave here.'

'My girl ... how did you −?'

He smiles. 'You ask Kamala to make a phone call, I think?'

'I ... no. I −'

'Ben, you must understand ... you *will* understand, that to ... to *accept*, is the only way to live − to survive. You look for more but I tell you, there is nothing − only accept and obey.'

I stare at the wall behind him, the jade-handled daggers arcing over his head − one of them has a horse head handle with flared nostrils and a red pinprick eye that glints in the light like it's alive. He raps the table. 'Look at me,' he snaps. 'Look at me.'

I turn slowly, look through him. A slick of hair oil is just visible on his temple. 'You will forget about England, about your girl. You work hard for me, there will be girls here to help you forget.'

I hear him swallow, hear the phlegm rattle in his throat and he lifts a delicate china vase and spits into it. Then he shouts a command, and from somewhere in the building, a door slams and in a minute or two, there are footsteps at my back and I turn to see her. She's dressed in turquoise silk and her hair is pulled into weird hanging plaits threaded with gold. Her blue eyes are ringed with black and her shoes look too big for her.

I go to her. 'Yun? Are you OK?'

She just looks at me dumbly, then at him. He gives a little laugh and crooks a finger at her. At once she goes to him and I watch as he takes her chin in his hands and squeezes. His fingernails make little red points in her flesh and I bristle. He's watching me closely.

He twists her chin to look at me. 'Your little friend,' he says. 'What do you think of her now? Look very good, I think?'

I look at the floor.

'She tried to get away but she know she can't hide from me – same as you, Ben. You run, I catch you. You do it again, I catch you again. You do it one more time and I will kill you. Understand?'

In my head I'm smashing his face into the marble. Over and over. My teeth are grinding in my skull but I manage to return his look and nod.

He smiles, leans back. 'You wanted to fight for this girl? You win for me against Mr Chai, and she stays, and maybe I give her to you – one night – reward.'

She doesn't move, she's still as a statue, her face set and as he speaks, he pats and paws at her. Now I know why he wanted to see me – to let me know he knew about the phone call, and to see Yun. To see her with him – owned by him – and to offer her to me like that meant something between us.

All he's done is make me more determined than ever to get out of here.

He gives her a final pat and she leaves us, and even though I don't see her go because I'm eyeballing Ping across the desk, I know she won't lift her eyes to look back at me. I know she's looking at her feet as they cross the floor, and the sound of them, soft and light, are all I hear. A door closes somewhere in the house and there's quiet. He leans forward and brings his little chicken-feet hands together so his fingernails meet with a click.

'So, you give me a good fight?' he smiles. 'Yun will be watching. You win, you make lot of money for me. Fight very soon. You get strong. You train. You eat. Big muscles. Good feet. Kick and hit very hard. Chai's boy very good kick boxing.' He chuckles. 'Only after,' and he gestures up away where she's gone. 'But if you lose, she goes to Mr Chai – to Thailand, forever. Understand?'

'Can I go now?'

He's quick as a fish, and before I even see it, I'm hit across the side with a cane that bends and whistles like a whip in his hand. 'I decide when you go.' He leans in again, breathing hard. I'm trying to stand up straight and the effort is making me cough. He spits the words at me: 'I told you: you killed my men – you owe me – you belong to Ping. I own you.'

I'm sent back soon after that and, as the car pulls out, I look up at the house and see Yun's face at a window. She's not looking at me. She's not looking at the car or the drive or the gates. She's just staring, and her face under all that make-up is pale and blank and sad.

He stands behind her, watching me leave.

11

I'm locked in the cell just two minutes before I'm hammering on the door. Lee doesn't come back at first so I pick up the chair in the room and I break it into matchwood. Then I start on the walls: I ball up my fists and throw punch after punch, and every time I pull away and there's grit and blood on my knuckles, I feel better and so much worse at the same time.

Lee hurries in and I roll into him and stagger back like I'm drunk. He holds me up and tries to help me to the bed but I struggle up so he sits back on his haunches and looks at me. 'What happened, Ben?' His eyes are wide.

I stare at him and shake my head. 'Ping,' I whisper. 'Ping. I am going to … to end him. I'm going to fucking kill him.'

He sighs, long and hard. I wipe the sweat from my eyelashes and then I sit on the bed and lie back to get my breath while he scratches at himself. 'What I wanted to say before … he is a … a very dangerous man – you don't know.'

'I can see that.'

'He never on his own ... and he is watching – all the time.'

I think about the phone call – how he knew – and the darkness, that blackness, is coming for me again but this time I don't even resist it. I want it. I want it inside me.

He shakes his head. 'You have to win this fight.'

'*What*? Why? Fuck, Lee, look at me,' I say. 'You don't understand, I'm telling you, I have to get out of here ...'

'I know you feel bad but –'

'*Bad*? You got no idea. But it's not even that … it's …' I can't begin to explain why. 'Look, if I can get the others to come …'

He shakes his head and the flesh on his neck shivers. 'Never. Too dangerous.'

'Then what?'

'You go. Alone. Get help. Tell someone – police – we are here.'

'I thought –?'

'Impossible. He is watching.'

'But you must go out, don't you?' I say, 'what happens when –'

'I am not allowed.'

I stare at him. 'What, nev –'

'Never. Mr Ping say he cannot trust …' he tails off miserably.

'Fuck,' I breathe. His eyes are wet. 'Why?' I say, 'why not?'

'I don't want to –' and he starts to cry – gulping and shaking.

'Hey, Lee. It's OK. You don't have to tell me … It's all right.'

He sniffs and nods. I can't deal with it. I've heard enough. So I just change the subject: 'What's this guy like – the one I'm supposed to be fighting?'

He swallows, looks up. 'Thai boy? Fighting name is Tiger.'

'He's got a fighting name? Shit.'

'Yes yes. Fighting name. He fighting long time. Very good. Muay Thai – in English, "Eight Limbs" … eight points, you know? Eight – eight way to hit: knee, shin, elbow, fist. Two each. Is very good in Thailand. He train long time. Very good.'

He fishes in his pocket and pulls out a picture of the Tiger. It's a grainy black and white snap off a promo flyer. Half of him is covered with writing but his face is clear: small and pinched, with hard, narrow eyes above a crooked nose. He wears a bandana around his head and his hair is plaited down his back. He's in classic fighting position, body tipped, one elbow pulled back about to strike and one foot raised in a kick.

'He looks hard,' I say.

'He is hard … but he tired too. Make many fight. Like I say, not hungry like you. Just tired. You are not fear of anything. And you are new fighter. This boy been fighting for Mr Chai in Thailand a long time. Train long time. He is like … old man inside. Old and tired. Looks good on outside but inside … dead. Want to sleep. Want to stop. He is like me,' he breathes out, 'prisoner too long. Scared to lose but scared to win.' He nods. 'You can win this fight.'

He's so wrong about me wanting to win: I don't want to win. I never wanted to win. All I want, all I've ever wanted, is to be let the fuck alone. And I don't know if that makes me "hungry" – I reckon all it makes me is a bit sad.

He snatches the picture from me, folds it carefully and stows it back in his pocket.

I push my back into the cool of the wall. 'Lee,' I say, 'Lee, look, I'm sorry but you don't get it – I don't care. I don't care about winning; I don't care about the fight.'

He blinks sorrowfully and his eyes fill, then he just hangs his head.

'Lee, please, don't. Don't get upset again. Just … just help me.'

There's a long pause and all the usual shouts and scuffs and clanging of doors seem to stop. After a bit, he drops his head and whispers, 'You only get out of here when you are dead.'

He looks at me intently, nods, then heaves himself up and I watch him leave.

12

That night I dream I'm buried: nailed in a box in the dark and the clatter of earth on the lid. Vines are growing through the box now and I clutch at them trying to pull it apart – but they're not vines at all –they're roses: thick whiskery stems, and thorns that hook in my skin.

I wake up in sweat and I know what I have to do – what he meant.

Outside, in the passage, the strip lights in the ceiling glow and dim and glow again. The walls are wet and pitted and marked with graffiti. The cells are quiet.

I have to die.

The roses: I remember the boy with the rose tattoo – the boy Rooster beat and finished – bundled out in a sack.

That has to be me.

All I have to do is bide my time. And trust that Lee's maybe desperate enough to help me to do it. I have to go along with it all – all this bullshit – look like I mean it, and wait.

It's a week till we get the chance to talk again.

I'm in the gym, circuit training with some of the other guys, and Lee's barking at me when the door swings open and Baby Face comes in. He looks pale and bruised but he gives us a smile. Rooster's been training but he stops and holds the punch bag to his chest. The boy with the ear missing halts mid-skip. Lee turns and I hear him take a sharp breath. His face is white. He leaves me and walks, and I stop what I'm doing and watch. He puts both hands on Baby Face's face, traces his lips with a fingertip, pulls him towards him and kisses him on the mouth. And Baby Face is there kissing him right back. Then they look back at us, suspended there under the buzzing strip lights and Lee shouts at me, 'Come on! One hundred circuit! I back soon!'

As the door closes on them, I turn to Rooster. He raises an eyebrow, shrugs and starts pelting the punch bag. After another couple of turns, I go to him. He's working up a sweat at the bag; his arms are running with it. I tap him lightly on the shoulder and he turns like he's been stung.

'Hey,' I say. The small boy with one ear steps up and Rooster waves him off. I nod to the door. 'When did he get back?'

'Today.'

'He's been in hospital?'

'Not hospital – Ping has doctor who works for him …'

'Why? I mean, why bother? He wanted me to kill him, for fuck's sake. I thought Ping didn't give a shit about –'

'For Lee,' he says simply. 'Lee begged him.'

'Christ. He had to beg him? To fix him?'

He shrugs.

I say, 'I didn't know him and Lee were … I mean I guess I didn't know Lee was –'

He swings the bag away from him a little. 'Lee likes boys.'

'Yeah.'

'Lee loves him. Was very sad when he was hurt – and after … Ping knew he had to do something.'

'What, or Lee would lose it?'

He shrugs. 'Maybe.'

I lower my voice. 'I asked him to help me get out.'

He pushes me up against the wall. 'You told him?'

I push him back and he bounces. 'What? I trust Lee,' I say, 'I trust him.'

He waits, leans in. 'You are a fool,' he says. 'In here you cannot trust anybody.'

'Whatever man,' I say. But there's a cold cramp in my guts.

He looks at me hard and runs his hands in his hair. 'Ping will kill you,' he says.

The small boy has stopped what he's doing and is standing pulling at his remaining ear watching us closely. He's the size of a ten-year old but he's all muscle, his hands are bound in dirty bandages and his hair stands up in spikes. I notice a couple of teeth are missing. He mutters something to Rooster who points at my back and translates: 'He says your tattoo – the snake – means good luck.'

The boy says something else and Rooster smiles and says, 'But he says snake eat rabbit. He was born in the year of the rabbit.'

I smile and shake my head. Just then the door opens and it's Lee, closely followed by Ping and Bao Zhi.

'Not training? Not working?' says Ping. 'You don't want win? Don't want little girl? Shame.' He chuckles, and I turn and grab a punch bag and hammer at it till my head spins.

Later that day when it's getting dark, I'm in the yard smoking. It's colder this evening and there's a dense smell of diesel and fried spice in the air. The other boys crowd together, a little apart from where I am, stamping the ground, sharing cigarettes. Rooster, the Rabbit, Baby Face, and three others: a tall, wiry boy with skin like tracing paper who scratches at dark blotches on his arms; a stocky lad called Wen; and a guy with a giant Buddha tattoo across his back. Behind us, a door opens and Lee schleps over in yellow sandals, scuffing up dust in his wake.

Rooster hangs back, pulling on the dregs of a cigarette. Lee nods and looks at me. His breathing's hoarse and he looks pale and drawn.

'Ben?' he says.

The others shift and twitch – I turn and catch Rabbit's eye. 'What?' I say. And they melt away.

Lee pats me on the back and I flinch – I'm so wired – so completely fucked by all this – I've almost forgotten what normal human behaviour feels like, what to do. But I know what I want – and that's all that matters right now.

I turn to face him. He's staring at me.

'What is it?' I say.

He looks over at the boys – and I know he's looking at Baby Face. He coughs out the words: 'I will help you.'

'Thank you.'

I'm aware of the others watching now. I lead him away towards the fence.

And when we're there I say slowly, 'Lee, what you said, the only way to get out of here is if you're dead, you remember?'

He doesn't say a word but a muscle in his face flickers and pinches the skin.

'You meant, I play dead – you get me out and I get help. Yes? I saw you once, lifting a body into the back of car – Do you know where they take them – do they dump them? Bury them? What do they –?' When he still doesn't say anything, I prod him. 'Lee?'

He nods. Looks back at the others. 'I am scared, Ben.'

'I know. Me too.'

'What he can do – what he will do if –'

'Once I'm out, you're all out. I'll –'

Rooster's behind me now. He locks his hand on my arm. 'Leave it,' he says. 'You are making trouble for everyone.'

I shrug him off and he comes round to face me, angry now. I force myself to speak, keeping my voice low. 'Listen, I don't want to fight you – I don't want to fight anyone anymore. All I'm saying is, I want to go home. You can all do what you want. I'm not telling you what to do.'

Rooster says, 'We've all tried –'

'Whatever,' I say, and to Lee, quietly: 'You'll help?'

He looks at me a long time – and I know the work he's doing – the weighing and measuring. He walks away and I follow. 'Lee?' I say.

He takes a breath, a long sigh, and looks across at Baby Face once more. 'Tomorrow.'

'Tomorrow? We can –?'

'Might, maybe work: you in the ring with Chang – you go down – you don't get up, you never move. I can carry you to car. Pay driver. He will get you out. I try to arrange.'

'Lee, that's –'

He doesn't let me finish. He turns to go, and then I see him freeze. I look over and see Rabbit switch, back away; the others follow fast, then disperse across the lot.

I turn in the direction of his gaze, then I see what he saw – first, the dogs – matted fur, broken claws, and their mouths pumping in the heat, and then Ping, standing by the door, half in shadow, his arms folded, and his fingers tapping up and down on his elbows. He moves his head into the light and he catches my eye.

He shakes his head very slowly.

13

Late last night I heard voices outside the cell. Ping's sing-song voice, and the nasal, mid-Atlantic whine of Mr Chai. Footsteps on concrete, and maybe Lee's laboured breathing I wasn't sure. I turned over, went back to sleep and dreamed about fighting: pushing my foot or my elbow into bone, the thud and the crack of it. And then I wake up, sharp – alert – like I'm still in the ring.

I see Rabbit on the stairs and he gives me the thumbs up, smiles. Lee's waiting for me. He's anxious. So anxious I can smell it on him: beads of sweat shine on his scalp and eyebrows. He rubs his palms together over and over, and little curls of dead skin shoot away from him like moths. Our eyes meet and he gives me a little nod.

Rooster's already in the ring, his face waxy under the lights.

I whisper to Lee, 'Does he know?'

He shakes his head. 'No. No one. Only driver.'

'You know I'm coming back for you – all of you?'

'Go on,' is all he says.

I shake off my shirt and climb in the ring with Rooster. Lee claps his hands and we start moving. I'm wired, buzzing, and I start into him straightaway. He picks up and comes back at me with fists and feet. Already, I can feel the blood singing in my ears. Lee's saying something from the ringside but I don't catch it. Rooster's circling me, looking for an opening, and it's then I look up for a moment and see beyond Lee: Kamala. She's watching intently – her hands locked in front of her. I don't know why but I stop – and when I think about it later, it was something about the way she looked at me that made me. Rooster slams into me and I go down. I hit the floor so hard I can hear my teeth ring in my head.

So. I don't get up. I don't move. I lie there.

Rooster's pumping his fists and cawing – he gives me the odd half-hearted kick in the ribs. I groan once, close my eyes, and wait. I hear Lee howl and hurry into the ring, I feel a rush of water on my face but I don't flinch, I don't move. Lee says something then, his voice cracking, and I can feel myself being lifted. I lie limp as I'm handed down from the ring and hoisted over a shoulder. I hold my breath, keep my eyes shut. I know we pass Kamala though because I smell her scent and for a second I open my eyes. She starts as she sees me, and I quickly close them again and hang my head as we go through the door and down the stairs to the cells.

More shouting from Lee, and the sound of footsteps dying. I open my eyes. I'm in another cell – one I don't recognise – there's a single light bulb hanging from a cord in the ceiling, and a wash of dried blood on the floor. In a corner is a pile of sacking. The smell of rot is fierce. I push on my elbows and shuttle back. 'Did we –?'

He pushes me back, puts a finger to his lips, and I lie still. More footsteps, more shouts from Lee and I'm lifted again. Then darkness: the scratch of sacking on my skin, dust and grit in my nose. I'm lain down again and I wait, hardly daring to breathe.

Screaming. Howling. More footsteps, and I fucking know it: Ping. I can just make him out through the weave in the sack. He's still yelling. Lee's voice then, pleading, sobbing. Then I see the shadow of Ping's cane as he brings it down over Lee's head and back, and I have to fight to keep my fists from closing. Lee's sniffing as Ping clip-clops over to where I lie and kicks me sharply in the ribs with his pointed boot. It wrings the breath from me. He delivers another then, and another, and all the time he's screaming. I see Lee struggle to his feet, still bent double, as Ping leaves.

It's suddenly quiet except for Lee wheezing and murmuring to himself.

'Lee,' I whisper. 'Are you OK?'

Not a word. He bends and heaves me onto his shoulder. The sack's straining over my head and I'm breathing rice flour and mouse shit. It's so tight, I can't move or twist in it and I lie slack as he hurries, puffing, across concrete and tarmac. There's the sound of metal gates scraping and a car boot being popped.

'Good luck,' he whispers.

I'm flung into the cavity and I fold up as the boot slams down. Dark. I let my breath out. I hear voices, indistinct, a car door opening and closing and the engine revving.

The car sets off and we're rumbling over the rutted ground outside the inner compound. Beyond it – beyond the lot – I know, are the main gates.

The car slows down. Then stops. We must be at the gate. Already I'm making plans.

I'm an idiot.

The door again. A short swell of voices and then a loud crack and a thud. The boot's opened and the sack is roughly torn off my head and body. I open my eyes. Three men are standing over the boot: one is the guy who chased Yun and me in the truck; the other's a tall, bony man with a broken nose. He's folding the sacking neatly, close against his chest. And in between them, is Ping. He's smiling.

'Ben,' he says. 'I told you – accept and obey. You did not listen to me. And now there are … consequences – there are *always* consequences.'

I haul out of the car and try to run but the tall guy's faster, and he grips on my wrist and pulls me back, brings me to stand in front of Ping.

'Come with me,' Ping says.

'What are you going to do?'

'You don't ask questions,' he spits. 'You don't have privilege to know anything. Not now.'

The men drag me between them after Ping, my head hanging and my feet brushing the ground. Through the gates to the inner compound where we smoked, where I talked to Lee, where the dogs pant and slobber. They jerk me to a halt.

I stand up and scan the lot.

Lee's there – his wrists are bound and he's kneeling in the dirt. And by the door, on the threshold, a figure is standing, arms folded: Kamala.

Ping lets me take it all in. Then he says, 'One more, one missing.' He leans up to the tall man and mutters something. The man nods, leaves me in the grip of the other, and disappears, past Kamala, who moves into the sunlight.

'Kamala,' I call, twisting in the man's hold. 'Get the others – get Chang! Hurry!'

She looks across at me, then at Ping.

He says to her, 'Come here.'

When she's close, he looks at me and says, 'You like this girl, I think?'

I say nothing.

'She is very beautiful,' he says. 'I know. She work for me a long time. She is very beautiful, and very … what do you say? … loyal.'

'What?' I say.

'I cannot be everywhere. So I must have help – eyes and ears in all places.'

'You mean …? Kamala? Did you –?'

She doesn't look at me. Ping says, 'Everyone has a price, Ben. Everyone can be made to change path – even you.'

'But …' I've got nothing to say.

'But, but, but,' he goes on. 'But … you trusted her? Mistake. Trust only yourself. And me. I don't change – I never change.'

'Lee?' I say miserably.

'Lee wanted to help you – feel sorry for you. But Lee is finished for me. He knows that. He knew that when he said he would help you. He is … dead man – just like you,' and he laughs. Lee's eyes flicker up, then down again. His face is white.

There's a commotion from the door – a high-pitched yelping – and I see Baby Face, bound and squirming, being pulled and shoved by the tall man. At once, Lee raises his cuffed hands and falls to the ground. Baby Face is pushed down beside him, with Ping directing all the time in Mandarin.

Lee's jerked up again and they kneel facing each other. Ping draws a pistol from his belt.

'NO!' I wriggle free, run at Ping and knock him to the ground. The gun clatters away in the dust and Ping scrabbles for it with his spider fingers. I go after it but I'm pulled back by the guy that was holding me, while the tall man helps Ping to his feet.

Lee and Baby Face don't move. They kneel together, their eyes on each other. One of the dogs looks up, its ears sharp.

The tall man hands the gun to Ping who spends a while scratching and picking at little scabs of dirt from his suit, looking up at me from time to time. The man has one arm around my throat and the other on my wrists behind my back.

'Don't do this,' I say. 'Fucking let them go. Whatever. You got me – you caught me – you'll get your fight, just let them go. This is on me, not them.'

He stops, a little knob of charcoal pinched in his thumb and forefinger. 'Ah. So you fight for me *if* I let them go?'

'Yes. Yes. I'll win. But I need Lee. I'm not ready yet. Lee, am I? *Lee?*'

Lee doesn't even shift. He's still looking straight at Baby Face. He's mouthing something at him – his lips are just moving – and I see Baby Face give a barely perceptible nod.

I call again, my voice brittle and shrill: 'Lee? What the fuck?'

Nothing.

'Mr Ping, please? I'll fight for you. I'm good – I know I can win for you. Please let them go?'

He slips out his pocket square and dusts the barrel of the gun, holds it up. 'Do you remember what I told you before?'

'I – I don't –?'

'Two words,' he snaps. 'That's all: accept. Obey.'

'Accept, obey. Right. Yes. I remember.'

'You remember ...' he says slowly. 'You remember, but still you try to make a bargain with me?'

'I don't –'

'You try to make a price, a bargain, but you don't have anything to bargain with. If I want you to fight for me – in my cages – to *win* for me,' he's shouting now, and I see Lee move his head in Ping's direction, 'then you *will* do that. Do you understand?'

'I do. Yes. I do, but ...'

'No "but".'

'No. OK. I accept. I obey. I need Lee to train me though. He knows Mr Chai's boy – how to beat him. He knows –'

'Maybe you right. Maybe Lee can live. For now. But what you do must be paid for – must be punished – and someone must pay.' And he raises the gun, points it at the side of Baby Face's head and fires. Lee screams and Baby Face slumps to the side, black blood pooling in a halo around his head.

14

Back in my cell, I can still hear Lee – a thin, pitiful crying that I'll never forget.

I won't forget Kamala's face either as Baby Face fell – how she gasped and stifled a cry with her fist in her mouth. And Ping, stowing the pistol and walking smartly back through the door without a look.

All I can do, all I can do, all I can do is end this – to make amends the only way I know: to do some damage.

I don't see Lee the next morning but I train like fuck – like he was there anyway – it's all I can do, I keep telling myself. Somehow, someway I have to make this fight matter.

No one speaks. Everyone knows. I keep my head down.

It's later, after I've eaten, that I see the Tiger. I'm in the yard smoking, keeping my distance from the others, when I see him – away behind the compound fence. Chai's with him, and a couple of big guys in dark track suits. He's smaller than me but he carries himself like a fighter, strutting with a pumped up chest under wide shoulders. I know he's young – Lee said he was about my age – but he doesn't look it. His face is lined: deep creases wrap his forehead, and his mouth is puckered and white. He steps up to the fence and watches us, shielding his eyes from the sun. I look straight at him but he's not there. He's wax: impassive, no thinking, no feeling. And I think about what Lee said about him being tired. And the life he's lived to make him look that way. A cold shiver goes through me and I turn and walk the other way.

Broken voice behind me: 'Ben?'

I go to him. He looks smaller, kind of boneless.

I say, 'Lee, Lee, I'm so sorry. I didn't –'

He shakes his head and looks at me. The whites of his eyes are pink and shot. 'I knew,' he says.

'I don't understand?'

He sighs. 'He is gone – but he is … he is safe. Ping can't hurt him anymore.'

I breathe. 'Fuck, Lee. I'm so sorry. I'm so – shit, I don't even know what to say.'

He's quiet for a minute. 'Say nothing,' he says. 'Do something.'

I hook my fingers in the fence. And I think about my father and the last time I saw him – and what I am – what's ticking inside me – and what I have to do. 'I will.'

He nods and turns to go, then thinks better of it and comes back. He rubs his hand over his mouth, lowers his voice and says, 'Before ... before this,' he swallows, 'I did not know how to be angry, but I think it is better to be angry. Better to do like you do. Better to fight back. Fight for what you love. I was too scared. But ...' his eyes widen. 'After this, I am not scared anymore.'

'That's good to hear, mate,' I say but nothing he says is ever going to make me feel OK about any of this. He digs in his pocket, brings out a greasy scarf and hands it to me.

'What's this?'

'To bring you luck. Was mine when I was fighting.'

It's not much more than a piece of torn cloth but coiled along the length of it, is a snake, its scales picked out in green and gold.

'Thanks,' I say. 'Thank you. I'll wear it.'

He nods. 'Like your snake tattoo.'

'Yeah. Yes, it is. Lee, I don't know what to –'

He shakes his head. 'Time to go.'

Two days, three days, in the ring with Lee and I'm ready – we're ready. I'm quick off the mark but I'm solid too. Balanced. I know when to use my heel or my shins. I can land an opponent with a blow of my elbow, pull someone off their feet and tear them up. It's going to be good – fireworks – because this is the last fight Ping's getting out of me or anyone else.

The evening before the fight, I see Rooster. We've not talked much since Ping killed Baby Face, since Kamala betrayed us. He's looked so fucking bleak since then – Kamala's disappeared – no one's seen her since it happened. He comes up to me in the yard.

'Hi,' I say.

He's rolling a cigarette so he doesn't look up. 'Hi.'

'You OK?'

He draws the paper across his tongue and shrugs. 'OK.'

The air's very still, thick and wet. I scuff the dust with my toe, say it fast: 'You still think you want to stay in here?'

He looks up through smoke, narrows his eyes. 'No,' he says.

'I'm going to try again – after the fight,' I say. 'But –' I hesitate, swallow, and his own words about not trusting anyone come back to me.

'What?' he says.

'This time I'm going to kill him.'

He flicks his roll-up away and grinds it. He gives me a half-smile. I say, 'We can bring a riot – all of us – just hammer him, his son, his men – burn the place to the ground.'

He's staring at me but there's a kind of light in his eyes.

I say, 'What we need is a place to hide out – after it's done.'

He says quietly, so quietly I don't even hear it at first: 'There is place.'

'Go on.'

'Yes. You know the building near the Freeway? Old? Burned up?'

The breeze blocked husk of a building opposite. I nod. 'Yeah. But it's too close. They'll find us.'

'Ah, no.'

'No? Why not?'

'Because under building … is …' he searches for the word and I almost stamp my foot.

'What?'

'Under the ground … like for train,' he says desperately.

'A tunnel?'

'Yes. But old. It goes underground. Into city.'

'OK. And he doesn't know – they wouldn't know?'

'No. They know nothing about that,' he spits.

'And how do you know about it?'

He blinks. 'I remember – long time ago – when I was a child, I slept in there. It was a safe place – still can be.'

'OK,' I say. 'OK. And you'll tell the others?'

He nods.

'Lee says he'll see to the keys. And then we need to –'

'We will do the rest,' he says. 'A riot.' His upper lip hooks up and I see the sharpened teeth like needles in the gum.

'Cool. I'll need to – '

He puts a hand on my arm, looks at me. 'Kamala –' he starts, 'she was –'

'You don't have to explain –'

He shakes his head. 'She was … she was … broken. *Used*. No more hope.'

I nod. 'I know, I know. It's OK.'

He says softly, 'We are all broken.'

I'm about to say something but I don't get the chance. He spins on his heel and walks away from me fast, his shadow dragging behind him.

In my cell, on the mattress, someone has left a little jade statue of the Buddha, his hands folded across his belly and his eyes closed in prayer. I close it into my fist when I lie down.

15

I'm still holding it when I wake in the morning. There are noises from above, up through the ceiling: a faint hum and movement – dull scrapes and thuds, then voices.

Lee's standing at the door, his keys in his belt. He stoops to unlock it and steps in. He hangs back a little, head low and his fingers hooking and unhooking.

I hold up the Buddha. 'Was it you left this?'

He nods.

'Thanks.'

He scratches himself and leans behind him. He brings up a tin pail and places it carefully on the floor between us. 'It is time,' he says. His voice is blank, flat. In the bucket there are bandages and oil. He kneels down and I sit up with my back against the wall. He takes the Buddha from me, plants it solemnly on the blanket. He starts to bandage my hands.

'Wait,' I say, and from my pocket I produce the scarf

he gave me with the snake on it. I wrap it around my head and tie it tight. 'What d'you think?'

He nods but he doesn't even look at it. He just flattens my hand and carries on binding till I'm done.

There's a long wait and it's a wait because I know he's wanting to say something. I can hear footsteps approaching along the corridor. He says quickly, 'You are brave man, Ben. I hope you find your way.'

I swallow. 'I have to.' We're talking in whispers.

'To UK?'

'I need to … yeah.'

'Your family not sick?' he says.

'I don't … I don't know. I hope I'm in time.'

He finishes and closes my hands in his. 'You will make them better I think. Make them happy.'

My father crashes into my head – bent back and lonely eyes. 'Happy,' I say, 'yeah. I'll try, Lee.'

Then we both look up. I smell him before I see him: Ping is standing in the room, pinching a handkerchief into his top pocket. His scent fills up the room – oily and cloying. Lee gets to his feet and bows his head.

Ping snaps at him and stands back while Lee scuttles out of the room – not so far because I can still hear him wheezing.

Ping turns to me. 'Stand up.'

Accept and obey. I do as he says.

'Bow to me,' he says, and waits. 'Better.'

I look at him. 'What do you want?'

'You are ready to win?'

'I told you I was.'

'Lee train you?'

'Yes. Yes. He was good.'

'And training finished?'

'Yes.'

'After this fight is over, he knows he will die.'

I swallow and bow. I'm biding my time.

'Good,' he looks me up and down. 'You are learning to obey.'

He trots out and I hear him call to Lee who comes back in. He watches and waits by the door until we can no longer hear Ping, then he turns to me and looks at me for a moment with red eyes.

'What is it?' I say.

He puts a finger to his lips then he digs into the long pocket in his trousers and draws out a curved knife about a foot long. The blade has been cut by hand into tiny teeth. He runs it lightly across his finger and a tail of blood springs in its wake.

I swallow. 'Jesus. This is for him?'

'For him. For Hong,' he's talking about Baby Face. 'And for me,' he says. 'After, doesn't matter.'

He turns to go. 'Chang has the key,' he whispers. 'Wait here for me. Not long.' Then he's gone.

The noise from above has died to nothing. And then out of nowhere, comes the thrum of a long low horn calling. I can feel my blood pounding under my skin. My tongue's like paper. I close down, close my eyes and try to breathe, and it hurts to do it but I think about Mum then; and Charlie, about Sophy, about Maurice. I even think about school – about the person I was and can never be again – all that anger and emptiness – and then how Sophy filled me up, made me better. And suddenly, when I might not see it again, how much all of it matters.

I don't know how long I lie there but Lee comes in and calls me to say they're ready. I walk to the bathroom and look at myself in the mirror. The air above me is still filled with the sound of the horn music from the cage room. My face has hardened along with my body. I look like a killer. I am a killer. And I'm ready to be one again.

The noise stops as I walk in.

The cage is ahead of me, and in front of it are placed five high-back chairs in a little semi-circle; the ladder-backs on the chairs make strange barred shadow patterns in the light on the floor. It's been swept and dust motes hang in the air like flies.

I look down at Lee's fat heels slapping in their sandals in front of me and I walk. There's no one in the ring. I haul myself inside, feel the rough canvas web under my feet, and I wait. Except for Lee and me, the room is empty.

Then a door at the end opens and a silent little procession files in: Mr Chai, Ping, Bao Zhi, and with them, Kamala and Yun. Lee bows low and backs away. I wait.

They take their seats. Kamala, blank-faced, smooths her dress under her and perches upright on her chair, Yun sits stiffly next to Bao Zhi while Ping crosses and uncrosses his legs. He carries a little ivory-topped cane that he holds across his lap. Mr Chai purses his lips and looks me up and down. There's a low table in front of them, laid with drinks and multi-coloured dishes piled high with snacks. Chai leans forward and helps himself to a glass of whiskey. He swills it in the glass before he downs it in one. Smiling.

The door on the opposite side is swung open then and the Tiger enters flanked by Chai's men. The group all turn to watch him and Chai applauds. It sounds stupid and empty in this quiet room. Tiger holds his fists in the air for a moment, bows to Chai, and steps up towards the cage. He looks like a champion. He looks like a winner. There's nothing of the hollowness I saw before. I feel it, he makes me feel it. I steel myself and wait as he climbs in. I can smell the liniment on him – sharp and heavy. When he looks at me, he seems to see inside me – what I am and what I'm scared of.

I look for Lee and he gives me the thumbs up, mouths, 'Good luck, Ben.' He ducks out and heads for the door. He looks back once, catches my eye, nods, then disappears back the way we came. Chai's men follow him out.

Ping claps his hands. He nods at me, at Tiger. He takes a drink and holds it up to us. The honey-liquid in the glass catches the lights over the cage.

'We want a good fight,' he says. Chai nods, says, 'No stopping, no holding back – we are here to be entertained. Understand?'

Tiger looks at him blankly – blinks once then hangs his head. I look at Yun but she looks through me with cold blue eyes. I think of Lee's serrated sword hooking and slicing at Ping's throat. Ping claps his hands once, and the fight is on.

In less than a second, the Tiger's into me, straight from the hip with a fierce kick that cuts me under my arm. I go to check it but I don't make it and I go down. I'm up before he has a chance to grind me and I follow with a sharp foot thrust that gets him in the stomach. I use my elbows the way Lee taught me. I get right in close and hammer him in the face. I see blood then: I've cut him. He dances back, smudging blood from his eyes but I'm on him again. I throw a heavy punch at his face and his teeth rock in his jaw as his head swings away from my fist. But he's quick, and with a punch like that I've left myself exposed. He spins and strikes with his shin against my chest, hard enough to split the skin. And it's the cut that sharpens me, there's a kind of excitement there. I'm burning with it: I want him to hit me, throw me, and I want to tear him apart. I reel back and then rally with an elbow jab to his face.

I don't care about anything else but this moment. Here and now. Me and him. It's all I can feel. Skin and bone and pain. And that pain starts to feel like something I want, like something I'm going to miss after all this. Every kick, every turn, and every hook, and there's something else in there too: I'm winning – I know I am. He's coming back at me and I can see he knows this way better than I ever will, when to drive, when to hold back – but Lee was right, his heart's not in it. He's breaking.

He manages a couple of good blows, one at my jaw. He comes in with a mid kick but I block it again with my shin. And it's then I hear it or maybe feel it: a soft snap in his leg and I know he's feeling it. I see him wince as he puts his foot to the floor. I spit blood and glance at Ping. He's licking his lips like a snake.

I go towards Tiger slowly, purposefully, I make it last. I spin it. He's backing away, every other step causing him to grimace in pain, and I put up my guard, checking him with right jabs. I choose my moment and throw all the weight in my body through my left but Tiger catches it and turns his back to me, pulling my arm over his shoulder. He yanks down hard on my arm and my body buckles with the pain. I manage to get him away from me with a knee to the back but my left arm is hanging useless by my side. He comes back at me, limping. I push the pain away, crook my right elbow and missile it at his head. He zigzags back and falls to the ground breathing hard.

I can hear Chai's voice screaming at him. I kneel on his chest and pull up his head by his hair with my good hand. I go to slam him into the mat when I catch his eye, narrow, dark with blood. I pause a moment and he gives a tiny shake of the head and I know it – he's finished. I let go and he falls back onto the mat, his mouth lolling open and slack.

Chai's at the wire shouting now. I lean back on my haunches and pull away. Back by the wall, I can see Lee's come in, and behind him, Rooster, edging slowly towards the circle of chairs.

Tiger moves then – a shudder that runs from his neck to his feet. His face under the blood is white. Chai pulls out his phone and climbs into the cage as I step down.

I lock it behind me – drive the padlock home, take the key and watch the lock swing. He doesn't hear it – he's bawling at Tiger and talking on the phone.

Ping is beaming and Bao Zhi's pumping him on the back. And when I look for Yun, I don't see her anymore.

And then, out of nowhere, she's there: standing behind them, they're still seated, chatting animatedly. She looks at me, her eyes blank – she's gripping onto something tightly. When I look up, I see Lee walking slowly but purposefully towards Ping. At his side is the serrated blade he showed me. As he gets closer, he breaks into a run and hurls himself at Ping with a guttural roar and brings the blade down on Ping's neck. Blood arcs from the cut at once and he paws at his throat to stem it, but as he does, Lee goes in again. He rains down blows on Ping's body until blood's draining from a thousand cuts. Lee's face is deathly pale – his eyes are bloodshot and his mouth is set – a thin drool of spittle hangs from his chin as he works the blade.

Bao Zhi's face is white – frozen – he seems unable to move. Yun still stands behind him. A moment passes and then, almost at some invisible sign, she raises her arm, and it's now I see what she's holding: one of the jade-handled daggers – the red pinprick eye of the horse-head gleams in her fist. She steps forward, reaches around and draws the dagger across his white throat. He clutches at his neck, gurgling, staggers to his feet, then drops to the ground.

My left arm is twisted and swollen. I hold it and it's hot under my fingers. I'm breathing hard from the fight – I'm not in this yet and I have to be. When I look for Kamala, she's nowhere to be seen.

I go to Yun. 'It's done. We have to go … Yun?' Her eyes are glowing, a wash of Bao Zhi's blood on her cheeks. Lee looks up, panting.

'Lee, where are they? The others?'

'Fire,' is all he says.

Chai is pulling at the wires on the cage, shouting – the lock is giving out. I see him fish in his pocket, hear the sound of a safety catch snap.

'Shit. Yun, come on! Lee!' I grab Yun with my good arm and look back for Lee.

And from nowhere – a smell of burning – faint, but unmistakable. I can taste it. Thin grey wisps hang in the air above us.

The door to the stairs is open, and from outside, from below, there's a crack of breaking glass and the landing beyond the door fills with a bright glow. The strip-lights above us spark and gutter. Another blast, followed by a thunderous splintering. There's a bitter, caustic smell, then a blue glow in the doorway – frantic figures of Ping's men pushing and reaching to get out. I see Rooster's frame silhouetted for a moment in the glare before he disappears.

I call to Lee and his head rattles round. He straightens up.

The air is hot and hazy and the light from the fire dims and flares. The dogs are barking somewhere far off. There's a tearing sound and a shot rings out and Lee falls back pulling Ping with him.

The floor shudders as they fall. I hear Lee's head hit the boards. Ping's lifeless body lies across him, dwarfed by his bulk – blood leaching onto his shirt. And all the while, a thick seam of smoke is snaking its way into the room. Yun's face is white against black silk, but the bodies are shrouded in smoke. For a moment, I see Chai standing above us, still locked in the ring, his pistol in hand, and behind him, the Tiger. And as I watch, the Tiger lurches up, rolls toward him and kicks him off his feet. Chai loses his balance, falls, and the gun spins across the canvas and lodges in the wire. I run but Tiger's there before me – he crawls for it, grabs it and, as I'm unlocking the padlock, he turns it on Chai and blasts him in the stomach. He drops down from the cage, leaves the door winging on its hinges, and Chai twitching and groaning. We look at each other and he nods once.

'We won this time,' he says. And disappears into the smoke.

I go to Lee. He lies there, face up, spread eagled on the floor, his shirt rolled up and a great apron of dimpled flesh exposed.

I hear a faint whimper. 'He's still breathing – we need to get him out.' I kneel beside him and I lug his head onto my knees where it hangs loosely, slap and pull at his jowls: 'Come on Lee, we need to go - come on, wake up.'

But Yun doesn't help. She's on her knees over Ping, rifling through his pockets, pulling out sheaves of bank notes, stuffing them into her dress.

Lee splutters and coughs for a moment and his eyes roll in his head. In desperation, with my good hand, I try to haul him to his feet but he's a dead weight. I try a second time but his body rolls away from me.

'Lee, please?'

He grunts at me. Yun looks on. She kneels down and puts a hand on his face. He opens his eyes for a moment and blinks. He makes a low guttural croak that seems to come from deep in his belly. He's dying.

'Lee?' I say.

He blinks again and I know he's listening. 'Lee, I'm sorry, mate. You were so brave. I'm sorry.' His eyes fill with tears. 'All of us. We'll all get out because of you. You did it.'

Tears wash down his cheeks but he's gone, his head dull in my hands. Yun puts a hand on my back. 'Must go.'

I'm choked. I won't forget him. I let his head drop to the floor and close his eyes, brush the tears from his face and stand up, and smoke seeps and leaks, and covers him quickly.

Up to now I've been too distracted to notice but I'm slowly starting to feel the effects of the fight: apart from my arm which I'm sure is broken, there are sharp pains in my left side and a dull ache in my guts. I close my bad arm across my chest, grab Yun by the hand and we run out of the room. It's dark, and as we climb, the stairs are filling with black smoke. We reach the landing but the door at the top to the outside is locked.

I'm aware of Yun tugging at my sleeve. 'This way. Back. Come this way.'

She's pointing back down the stairs through the smoke, past the fighting room towards the cells.

'No,' I say and I'm hammering on the door, 'the others must have gone this way.'

'No,' she says, 'there's a way. Come.'

'Yun, no there isn't. Yun!'

But she's already turned and is spinning away round the curve of the stairs into the blinding smog.

'Yun!'

There's nothing for it. I drag my body around and follow her down into darkness. I'm coughing into my fist and I'm calling for her in the black.

'YUN!'

The crackle and hiss of fire in the cells – I can't see anymore. My nose and mouth are burning.

'Yun! For Christ's sake!' I'm waving my good arm about in front of me like a mad crab, shouting for Yun and I can't open my eyes any more, the smoke's so bad. It's everywhere: above us now, sucking and chewing at the air and then I hear something – a banging: fast, heavy slaps of metal on metal. I limp towards the sound. Holding my arm against my side, I move through the smoke, and every so often I pull to a stop to listen. After the third stop, I know where she is.

The bathroom is along a short corridor off the main one where the cells are. There's a milky beam of light coming from inside. I turn into it, still choking, my throat raw with coughing. The light comes from a strip in the ceiling but it's losing power: it fizzes and brightens then dims overhead. And in the light through the smoke, I see a small dark figure crouching on the wet floor, her arms raised.

'What are you doing?'

In her hand is a pointed shard of glass, and on the end of the point hangs a large round metal grille.

'What the …?'

She points down into a dark drain about two feet in diameter. She looks up at me.

'How I got out before,' she says simply.

Smoke licks around us. I crouch next to her, coughing.

'It's too small. Too small for me.'

She shakes her head. 'It's enough. Is bigger after. Come on.'

'Where does it –?'

But she's slipped away from me into the hole. I look back at the door to the room and a thick curtain of smoke bellies from the ceiling. There is no way out but this. I wait a moment and dive in, pulling myself along with my right arm. Wet earth, dirty water and rough concrete: we're in some kind of pipe. Yun's ahead of me, her little feet pumping and pushing against the sides. The pipe bends away and I lose her for a minute. It seems to narrow a little and my shoulders rub and crunch against it. My broken arm is burning and swollen, and deep inside it, at the heart of the break, the pain is huge. It's pulsing like an engine, hammering its way along blood and bone into my brain.

We're in total darkness now as we get further away from the bathroom above. There's still a thin tail of smoke following us, and my lungs are full of the stuff. Yun's far ahead now, pushing like a little mole and, slowly, very slowly I find I can see again. There's a tiny pin prick of light at the end and I pick up speed. The concrete tears at my skin but I go on, following Yun, moving towards light.

16

Sophy

When I come to, it's dark again. I've been asleep for hours but I'm not rested. My hands are crunched into fists and the muscles in my neck are twisted tight up into my head. And when I rub my eyes, they're wet with tears.

'We're very sorry,' they said. 'She didn't make it. She fought but …'

Trying to grasp it, the sense of it – it's like magic, like mist – like a thing close and far away and you can't measure the distance from where you are.

I'm lost.

Lily's everywhere. She's in the room: in the lights above me, folded into the sheets, curled around the door frame.

People talk all the time about I can't bear this or that, but they hardly ever mean it. "Can't bear the traffic or the rain or some celebrity", or whatever … but bearing something: really bearing it, like an old donkey under a ton of stones? That's what bearing really means doesn't it? Bent double under the weight of something that's crushing the life out of you. Bent so you can't take a single step further except that you have to. Bent so that all you can see is your feet under you and a square of pavement. That's what this is. And I cannot bear it.

I have to get out.

A knock on the door then and a figure in scrubs and a mask comes in with food on a tray. I'm shaking my head before she even gets to the bed. 'I don't want it.'

She's impassive. Controlled. Why should she care?

'I'll just leave it here. You might want it later.'

'Whatever. Where's my Mum?'

'Sorry.'

'Sorry? Sorry what? What does that mean?'

I see her eyes over the mask. Is that pity?

She shrugs and backs out.

I push myself up in the bed and the room spins and lights fur my eyes. Slowly I get out of bed and stand up. The floor's icy under my feet. Lily comes at me out of nowhere. I never thought losing someone would be like this. I guess I thought it would be quiet, creeping. But this: this is like being hit by a steam train. Every time. Every time. I need to talk to someone, be next to someone, and I think of Josh.

I go to the wall between the rooms, and I tap lightly at first, then louder. No answer at first and then a return tapping. But it's coming from a different place. I turn and he's at the window, his hand raised, looking straight at me. He levers the door and steps in. And he stands there, just inside the door. Still, his hands locked together in front of him. 'I just heard,' he says.

I feel salt in my throat and the tears boiling up under my eyes. I shake my head and sniff. 'You shouldn't be in here. They'll …'

'They'll what? I don't give a fuck. Come here.'

I go to him then and he's holding me, and he whispers through my hair. 'Sophy, you're so good. I'm so sorry. I'm so sorry this happened. I can't imagine what you're –'

'Don't. Please. Don't talk …'

I bury my head against his chest and he lets me cry. He doesn't try to stop me or try to comfort me. All I get is his heart, a slow, soft drum from deep inside him. And us – him and me – and for a single moment that can be OK. It's enough. Just for a moment. And later, I raise my head and he leads me to the bed and we sit there and his arm is still around me and I say, 'I want to see Mum and Dad. I need to –'

A silence then and he lifts my hand and pushes it against his. 'Didn't they tell you? Didn't anyone say anything?'

Blackness. Coldness. Blind terror. I scream at him. 'What? Tell me what? No! Please! No!'

I pull air into my lungs. Lily curls herself around me like a cat. 'What?'

'They've ... they've ... I can't believe no one said anything –'

'Josh? *What?*'

'They ... were ... taken. Today. I heard the nurses talking. They had the police here ... they'd have got to you if they could –'

'Taken?' He doesn't meet my eyes. 'Taken where? Who's "they"?'

Slowly he says, 'I ... I'm not sure.'

'What d'you mean? What? Well where are they? Where have they gone then?'

He closes my hand in his and looks away. 'Have you heard of the Reapers?'

'No. *Who?*'

'It's a kind of ... I don't know ... vigilante group. They're all over the South East. People who've jumped ship, broken through the road blocks ... living rough, you know. They're armed ... Some of our lot even joined them. They're a kind of underground group who've cut themselves off from –'

'What's that got to do with –?'

He squeezes my hand. 'Look I'm sure it's –'

'What Josh? Please tell me?'

'The Reapers ... well ... they ... don't wait. You know ...'

'What? Wait for what?'

'They don't wait for the all clear. If you've been in contact with someone who's had this then ... well, like I said, they're armed. They take people they think might ...'

And he tails off but he's done it. He says quietly, 'I've heard of it happening in other places. They … they just stalk the hospitals, anywhere … hide out … they …'

'No.'

'But you know, maybe I got it wrong, maybe your mum and dad are at home waiting for you …' But his voice is cracked and hollow. 'They're idiots. Nutters. Religious head cases. They think this sickness is some kind of … judgement. I don't know …'

'Is that supposed to make me feel better?'

'Shit, no. Sorry. No.'

I breathe. I'm alone. I'm all alone. It's like a bad taste in my mouth. Like a bad smell. Like something died in the walls. He leans in then. 'People are scared. You know. I've seen it. When they're scared they don't think straight. They go crazy. I'm sure it'll be OK.'

'Yeah.'

'Sophy?'

'Yes. Yes. I'm sure. I'll just wait here.'

I pull my hand away and shrug him off. Lily again. I close my eyes against her.

'Come with me?' he says.

I look up at him. 'Come with you where?' I say dumbly.

'I think we should get out of here. You got the all clear.'

'How d'you know?'

He points to my left arm. There's a small blue rubber band snapped around my wrist. He shows me his own arm with the same band. 'They must have put it on when you were asleep. You're OK to go.'

'Go where?' I say again.

He looks at me. 'Wait here. Sophy? Wait here? OK?'

I stare at the wall and blink twice. I feel like everything I'm doing is a kind of conscious act, even breathing. It's like bending back a stiff lever. Every time. And when I look up, he's gone.

I have to get out. I have to be outside. I'm thinking slowly. I need clothes. I need to brush my hair. I need to clean my teeth ... I ... need to ...

On the floor is the letter – the one I wrote to Ben – folded carefully. It must have slipped out when I was sleeping. I bend to pick it up and pull it into my fist.

The door opens then and he comes in with a bag of clothes. I don't know where he found them and I don't care. I stand in the middle of the room like a child, my arms stiff by my sides, the letter closed in my palm, while he closes the blinds and turns up the light. I can feel tear tracks on my face. I can't seem to make a sound. He comes to me, takes my hands in his and bends his head to look at me. Very gently he smudges at my cheeks with his thumb and folds my hair off my face and down my back. 'Sophy? Sophy?' he's saying. 'Listen, I got some clothes. OK? I'm not sure about the ... you know ... the size. I hope ... I found them in the laundry thing. They're clean,' he adds. 'Sophy?'

I know he's talking. I'm hearing the words but I can't fit them together. 'Sophy. Clothes? You going to get dressed?'

I stare blankly at him as he holds the bag. For the longest time we stand there and my body and my brain won't work, won't let me move. He opens the bag and pulls out a T- shirt, white, clean, folded. 'Sophy, put this on?'

I can't do it. He leads me back again to the bed and I sit down while he lifts my arms and takes my hospital gown off. Looking straight at me, he pushes the T-shirt over my head and pulls it down. I'm crying now and he stops and holds me, whispering softly in my ear, 'It's OK, It's OK. Come on Sophy. Jeans now. Come on …'

He helps me step into them. They're way too big for me and he pulls off his belt, loops it through and buckles it tight. When I've got my shoes on, I stand up, and I fall down again like a rag doll. I've lost my bones. And my heart. I lost my heart. 'I'm sorry. I can't … I just can't …'

'Come here.'

He bends and picks me up like a child, cradled in his arms, and opens the door and we're on the ward. Nobody stops us, nobody talks to us. My eyes are tight shut and it's only when I feel cold air singing in my face that I know we're outside. He shrugs me up into his chest and walks and all the time he's talking: 'It's OK, you're OK … I'm here. It's OK …'

He carries me home.

The first thing I see is the writing – huge black letters painted across the garage door:'PUNISHED'. It makes me gag. Josh sets me down and I hold onto the gate.

'They're going to kill them, aren't they?' I say.

He's walking towards the house and he turns and comes back to me.'Sophy, just try to be strong. Just stay here. I'm going to check out the house, OK?'

'Why? Why? I want to come.'

'Just wait here OK. Please?'

'OK. Fuck. OK.'

And I wait in that empty road by the gate by my Mum's lavender bushes and the white sheet waves and billows. I wait.

Josh comes out then and gives the thumbs up and I follow him in. The front door is open and there are footmarks down the hall. All the cupboards in the kitchen hang on their hinges like the wings of birds. Whoever it was has cleared them completely. Other stuff's been taken too but I don't care. I can't care. It's just what people do these days. What people expect. Everyone and everything is broken now. Josh busies himself barricading the front door and windows.

But in every room, on every stair, Lily's waiting, filling the house with herself: her toys and teddies and dolls and shoes and hairbrushes and her drawings. The smell and the words and the rhyme of her. I can't cry anymore right now. I sit down at the kitchen table. Josh comes in from the garden with a handful of leaves, and pushes a chest of drawers against the back door.

'All I could find. Mint. We have it all the time in the barracks. I can't even remember what real tea tastes like anymore. Did they take much?'

But I'm not really paying attention. He searches in the back of cupboards for something to boil water in and when he emerges with a tiny pan, he turns to me and says, 'This thing has to end soon Sophy. It has to burn itself out.'

And then I remember, and I know Charlie told me not to tell, but since nothing matters anymore, that doesn't either. 'You know what,' I say, 'this isn't just a virus.'

He looks up. The sharp sweetness of mint fills the kitchen. I go on. 'It's deliberate.'

'Eh?'

'Ben's brother told me. He found out. It's an attack – terrorism.'

'What?'

'North Koreans, I think. They're … it's a manufactured virus. Germ warfare. If they don't get what they want, they'll kill us all.'

He stares at me. 'What the …? How d'you know all this?'

'I told you, Ben's broth –'

'Alright, how does he know all this?'

I shake my head. 'I don't know.'

He crosses to the window. 'Why isn't this public knowledge then?'

'I don't know. I guess they want to keep a lid on it, stop people going mad …'

'Have you told anyone else?'

I shake my head.

'Fuck, Sophy. That's … that's deep. I can't take it in. So we're being attacked? This … this is what killed your sister, this is an attack, a weapon?'

'That's what he said.'

'Jesus,' he breathes. Just then his radio goes. 'Sarge? Yes sir. Yes sir. Still in hospital. Waiting for results. Yes, sir. Any news? Right … yeah, yeah … I'll let you know.'

He smiles and pockets the radio. 'They want to know what's going on. I told them …'

I smile weakly. 'I know. I heard.'

He turns back, pours the tea, brings it over and crouches in front of me. 'Look, I can't think about this tonight. And you … you must be shattered.' He waits a moment then he says. 'D'you want to go to bed?' and I know he doesn't mean it that way, I know he's just being nice, but it sort of comes out of his mouth and turns into a proposition and hangs in the air between us. He looks away blushing. And it's a moment or two till he can face me, and the clock on the cooker is ticking, and it's pitch black outside. Sleeping with someone – I mean sex – is the last thing I want right now, but *being* with someone when he seems to be the only person in the world who seems to care what happens to me … well. He takes my face in his hands and looks at me. 'I didn't mean … I meant …'

'It's OK,' I say gently. 'I know. But yes. I would like to go to bed.' He stands back to let me up and then we're standing together. I take his hand in mine and I say, 'Come with me. Stay with me. I don't mean ... to ... I can't ...'

He stops me. 'God, Sophy. I know. I understand.'

I close my eyes as I lead him up the stairs. Into my room. My bed. We undress in silence and he looks away when I climb into bed. Slowly, I lift the cover and he slides in next to me. A pale moonlight comes through the skylight and falls across his face. He turns on his side to face me. 'Sophy, I ... I know you don't ... it's just that I want to ... I want to take care of you. Look after you. I feel such an idiot saying it but you're ... you're beautiful.' I watch him, his dark eyes widen, then: 'It's not a line. It's not. Believe me. I just mean ... I never had anyone to ... I never felt like this, like I wanted to do this before – take care of someone. But with you ...'

'Josh, it's ... thank you. Thank you.'

I can't say anymore because I don't trust myself not to cry, but I turn on my side and feel his arms around me, his body warm against mine and slowly, very slowly I fall asleep.

Early light and birdsong wake me and then a crushing, crucifying sadness because she's gone and I'm alone. Josh is fast asleep but he stirs as I sit up. I try not to think about Ben and me here in this bed and his leaving. And what he might or might not be mixed up in. The letter's under my pillow. I take it out. It's warm where I slept on it.

'How are you? You sleep OK?' he says rubbing the sleep from his face and suddenly it all seems somehow twisted and wrong that he's here with me, getting inside my grief and my sadness. My loneliness. I was weak and that's something I can't afford to be. I get up and go into the bathroom and lock the door. We don't get water every day but today there's a thin trickle from the shower head. I stand under it until it dies with a gurgle. I know what I need to do.

I'm going to look for Maurice.

17

It seems to take forever but finally I see Yun slip from the end and light fills the tunnel. 'Come on,' she calls.

With one last wrench, I grasp the end of the pipe with my good arm and heave my body free into a slow moving channel of dirty water. It's thick with silky nests of green weed and rubbish. Up ahead a pink sofa bobs up and down like a drowned hippo.

Yun is on the other side on her knees, leaning in, her arms outstretched. 'Quick. Water very bad! Poison! Get out quick!'

I wade through the slime to the side. I'm waist deep and I can feel a sucking ooze under my feet. Yun grabs my arm and steadies me against the push of the water. When I'm ready, and with Yun helping, I heave myself out and lie on the side, my face in the ground, breathing in the water-stench off my clothes.

I get up. We're looking at a high fence behind which six lanes of traffic steam past at speed. Beyond it are the high rises and thick red haze of what must be the city. Behind us, I can see the fence around the compound and black smoke coughing from doors and windows. The fence has been trampled. To our right, up ahead is the place we want – the place Rooster told me about.

Keeping low, we pick our way over broken concrete and twists of wire, with Yun a few steps ahead, and duck through a wide doorway into the cool dark of the building. At once, every trip, every breath, is amplified a thousand times. We're only a little way in when Yun stops and puts a finger to her lips. 'Listen!'

It's very faint, so much so that I dismiss it at first, but then I catch it: voices, agitated whispers and the tip tap of feet from underneath us. She turns to me with wide eyes and I see her white fingertip as she points the way. We move slowly across the floor looking for an opening, a stairway, a way down. We cross burned-out hallways and cavernous hangers full of rubble and blackened timbers but there's nothing. When we stop next, the voices seem to be directly underneath us. She starts to tap at the floor with a stone. Soft rhythmic taps: one, two, three, and then a pause and then repeated like a kind of Morse code. I kneel next to her in the dark gripping my arm against my chest.

Over and over she repeats the drum and we listen, holding our breath, and it's there: stone on stone, tap, tap, tap, from far below us. We look at each other and she feels for my hand and her skin is ice cold. I let myself breathe.

'They're coming,' I say.

She nods.

We wait, crouching low, close together, the rank weeds from the drain drying on our skin and she whispers, 'Thank you, Ben,'

'I didn't do it. You and Lee did it.'

'You made it happen. You made me … hope … hopeful.'

'I'm glad.'

'What will you do, Ben?'

'I'm going to find a way to get home. And you?'

'I don't know. I will –'

But she's interrupted by a sound from behind us. We turn to see Rooster coming towards us. I jump up. 'Good to see you! We couldn't find –'

'Where is Lee?' he says.

'He didn't make it. He was so fucking brave.'

Rooster hangs his head. 'Ping?'

Yun nods.

'Dead. Lee killed him.'

Rooster smiles. 'Kamala?' he says it quietly, like he's ashamed of the word.

'I didn't see her,' I say. 'She must have got away when we were … she must have …' and I tail off because his face is kind of twisted. Yun is stiff and straight-backed watching him.

'I'm sorry, mate,' I say.

He shakes his head. 'Come, come, we can go. Follow me.' He takes off, moving lightly through the rubble down a dark passage that winds away from the corner of the room, so dark I hadn't noticed it before. We have to duck and dip around broken joists that cross our path. Then Rooster stops so suddenly I nearly run into him. At the end of the passage is a small low door.

It's so low I have to bend double which squeezes my arm and it's all I can do not to howl with the pain. The door is at the top of a metal staircase that corkscrews away into blackness. Rooster bends and heaves a large joist against the door to close it against intruders. He turns to us. 'Stairs very … bad … very broken. Slowly.'

He starts the descent, winding away from us in the dark. Yun goes next, and I follow up. It takes forever because we each have to watch and wait for the person in front to go at least ten steps. The treads are narrow; some are splintered into fragments; some are missing completely. We spiral down and down until I hear Yun gasp: down below are two thin points of light like cat's eyes. They move and flicker and as I descend I can hear whispering and movement from below.

At the bottom, I drop into freezing water up to my ankles. A flare from a match goes up and I see the boys huddled together under a low arched roof of black brick that runs with water. The Rabbit sloshes across to me and pumps my hand; behind him the other boys nod and grin.

There's a tunnel leading away from where we're standing and, hunched over, we all follow Rooster a few metres through it to where it opens out again into another low space but dry this time and lit by a small fire that sends mad shadows leaping and vaulting against the curve of the ceiling. Yun runs to the fire and kneels, stretching out her arms, her face lit and glowing.

'The fight?' Rooster says. 'You won.'

I shrug. 'For what it's worth. Poor fucker. He shot Chai – killed him I think.'

He nods, watching me in the firelight glow. 'I don't want to fight any more,' he says.

'I know.' We're silent, watching Yun tease and prod at the fire with little sticks. Her silk dress is ripped and fraying down one side. I shift my weight and cradle my arm as I do so.

'Your arm?' Rooster says.

'I think it's broken.'

He bends and pulls his shirt off over his head and starts to tear it into strips. The others are at the fire with Yun, and Rooster calls to Rabbit who fetches a short piece of wood to use as a splint and carefully they bind it to my arm with Rooster's shirt.

When it's done and I've thanked them, and Rabbit's back at the fire cross-legged next to Yun, their shadows merging on the vaulted ceiling, I say, 'What's the plan? What are you going to do?'

He sighs, turns to look at me. 'We want to stay together – go North. Far away.'

'How will you –?'

He looks at me and shrugs. 'We walk. Walk at night.'

'Jesus. But Ping's dead. He can't hurt you now. Why not stay here? Get work?'

His eyes are cold. 'You think we safe here? You crazy? Ping is dead but he has many friends. Only way to be safe is go far, far away. We go early tomorrow.'

He's right. I look across at the others. Some are getting ready to sleep, twisting and turning on the hard floor. Yun is still sitting with Rabbit who has his arm around her, watching the fire. Wen and the Buddha boy are playing a game with stones. The others are talking in soft whispers. I motion to a tunnel leading off to the right. 'And that's the way out?'

He nods. 'All the way. Take you under the freeway into the city.'

I turn back to Rooster and hold out my hand. 'Good luck.'

It's ages before he takes it but he does and he looks me in the eye and says, 'And you, Ben.'

I should leave it there but I don't. I can't. 'I'm sorry about Kamala,' I say.

'What do you mean?'

'Sorry she … sorry it didn't work out. I know you liked her, I know you –'

'And you?' there's a snarl in his voice.

'She's … she was … Yeah, I liked her. You knew that. But nothing happened. I told you, I've got someone back home. Sophy.' Saying her name out loud fucking kills me and I wish to God I never had.

All I get for it is a look.

Much later, the fire is dying red and white. Bodies sleep against bodies and the sound of low breathing fills the space. I can't sleep. I can't stop. I don't think I'll ever stop now. There's a ticking in my head telling me I need to go. I creep over to where they lie and pinch Yun gently. She's curled up, her hands under her head. She's awake at once and gets to her feet and follows me to the edge of the room.

'Yun. I'm going now,' I say. 'I have to go. Will you go with the others?'

She blinks and pulls her hair. 'Yes. I will go. Go for a while. I think it's maybe not safe to go to my aunt now,' she says slowly. 'Where are you going, Ben?'

'Home. Home to England.'

She reaches out and strokes my hand. 'In my life I have known many bad men. Many. You are good man. You will be lucky.'

She sounds like she's a hundred years old.

'Be safe, Yun. I'll think of you.'

'Me too.'

I hold her for a minute and then send her back to the fire. I take one more look around me and creep across to where the tunnel mouth yawns. It's low. Lower than the last and I have to bend right down to get through. It's held together with brick and timber struts. And it's dark. And wet. I inch along feeling my way with the flat of my hand. Stones roll and crunch under my feet and water drips down my neck. I've been in the tunnel for only a minute or two when I hear something behind me. I stop and push myself against the side and wait. There's a soft rustle and a splashing and I hear breathing. Yun.

'What are you doing here?' I whisper.

She comes up to me, pulls my good arm and opens my hand. 'For you,' she says and a little scroll of bank notes is wedged into my fist.

'No,' I say, 'You keep them, you'll need them.'

'I have more,' she smiles. She brings out the jade dagger from behind her back. It shines with its own light. 'I will sell this – very valuable.'

'You're brilliant,' I say, almost laughing.

She reaches up and strokes my face. 'Good bye. Good luck, Ben. I hope you find your home.'

I'm standing, water lapping at my ankles, and I bend and hold her to me. She blows a soft kiss in my ear and then she's gone, back through the darkness, and I turn and blunder away, my head down and my feet wet and sore but my spirits higher than they've been in a very long time.

18

Sophy

Josh is in the kitchen when I come out, with a couple of eggs boiling in the pan. 'Breakfast?' he says brightly, like everything's suddenly alright.

I shake my head and go to sit down.

'You OK?' he says.

I look at him. 'Er … no. Do I look OK? Is there anything about what's happened to me in the last couple of days that might make you think I'd be OK?'

He looks shocked and I feel better and then much worse. I'm being a cow. 'Sorry. Sorry.'

'No, no … it's OK. My fault, stupid question. I just meant … you know …'

'Yeah. I know. Thanks. I will have an egg if one's going.'

'It's good you got chickens. My Dad tried it for a while when it first started but they all died.'

'What does he do for eggs?'

'Trades stuff, he's a plumber. Useful.'

I nod.

'What about your Dad?' he says.

'He worked with computers, sales and stuff. But when they locked us all down – you know – after London, he couldn't travel. He basically … well, I don't know really. Grew stuff, kept chickens. Like everyone else I suppose.'

He brings the eggs to the table and sits opposite me, leaning on his elbows. He takes a breath and then: 'You know, Sophy, I meant what I said last night, about looking after you. I want to help you. I …'

I look at him and I know he's good and I know he means it. I knew last night but I just don't know what to say. All I want is to not feel like this anymore, ever. I hold his hand and say, 'Thanks Josh. I know. I can't … I just can't … you know, feel anything just now. I'm … I just feel … empty.'

He nods earnestly and squeezes my hand in his. 'It's OK. I'll stay with you. I'll stay here with you. We need to get some food in. I can see what I can get hold of –'

'Josh, you can't stay here. You're in the army. You need to get back. I'll be OK.'

'No. No way. I'm staying here. Not after what's happened … I'm not going to leave you alone.'

'Josh. Please? I'm OK really. Anyway there's something I need to do … someone I need to see.'

'Who? I'll come with you.'

'It's OK. Look, come and see me later if you can. You need to get back – you're probably in loads of shit for this. I don't want to be the cause of more hassle. OK?'

He leans back and looks at me. I get up from the table. 'I'm going to get dressed. If they've left any clothes.'

He stands up and comes and puts his arms around me, and I have to tell myself to lean in, to hug him back, accept what he's giving me, but I just can't do it. I stay stiff, brittle, in his arms until I feel his lips brush soft against my neck. I pull back at once. 'Josh. Please.'

'OK, I'm sorry. I'm going. But please don't switch on any lights and barricade yourself in? Can I see you later? Come over later?'

'Give me a call.' I'm halfway up the stairs now, and I can feel him hesitate and dither.

'Who is it you're going to see?' he says.

I can close my eyes and I'm back there in Maurice's room, the blue screen light and the old Alsatian. And Ben, Ben, Ben. Both of us wet from the rain, covered in mud and scared and my hand in his.

'Someone I used to know, that's all.' And I turn and go to my room, and a minute later, the front door bangs, and from my window I see him walking away down the street, his shoulders set and his fists clenched at his sides. And I go and lie down on my bed and I sob my heart out.

Whoever was in here, was in my room too. I hadn't noticed anything last night but someone's been in

here. Stuff is in different places, some stuff is missing.
I'm reaching on the top of the wardrobe for a bag
when I come upon Dad's shotgun. It's right at the back,
against the wall, and next to it, under my fingers, I find
a small cardboard box that rattles with bullets. I take the
gun down and hold it in my hands, feel the weight of
it – the cold of the barrel and the wooden heft of the
butt. And a cold shiver runs through me.

I load it and lock it and I hide it.

I dress quickly and go out. The sky is thick with grey
clouds and there's an icy damp in the air as I walk into
town. There are road blocks everywhere, and ahead of
me, up on the London Road, a convoy of army trucks
rumble by. There's a car dealership on the corner of the
London Road with a dozen cars long since abandoned
on the forecourt, their windows smashed and the bodies
sprayed with paint. I duck in across the forecourt and
bruise through a hedge of hawthorn bushes at the back.
Beyond them, is a low wall that backs onto the alleyway
where I first met Maurice.

Weeds, three-foot tall, sway and paw at me as I go
down the alleyway. There are banks of uncollected
rubbish sacks against the walls on either side where
sleek rats are foraging. Someone's dumped a fridge
freezer here, its door gapes open and a tongue of black
resinous fluid licks into the corners. I have to hold
my breath against the smell of rot: heavy and sweet, it
comes at me in waves and by the time I reach Maurice's
door, I'm gagging.

There's a large cardboard placard loosely tied to the railings outside his place with the words: KEEP OUT OR GET SHOT, scratched in black. I climb up, and knock and wait.

I wait for ages on the step, I know there's someone in there, I can hear him. I make out a bulky shape through the net curtains. After a while, I knock again and there's silence and then a muffled, 'Fuck off!'

I lean into the letterbox and shout: 'Maurice? Maurice? It's me, Sophy. I'm a friend of Ben's? Maurice?'

A long silence, then a mad kind of muttering that sounds like a pack of angry squirrels, and after a bit, I hear bolts being drawn and chains pulled and the door is opened and he's on the step.

He's Maurice but not Maurice. He's much, much thinner than he was; his cheeks are hollow and his eyes have drilled down in their sockets, and when he goes to speak, I see half his teeth are missing. There's a smell coming off him, rank, like mould. His eyes narrow and I know what he's looking for. I hold up my arm to show him my wrist band. He squeezes his cheeks back into a grey sort of smile. 'Sophy? Alright then?'

'Um … I'm … I'm OK. You?'

He looks at me and shrugs. 'Been better.'

I nod. 'Actually, me too.'

He scratches at his beard. What's up?'

I force myself to say, 'Maurice, would it be OK to come in? I wanted to talk to you.'

He hesitates, pushing a slippered toe over the

threshold and back and grunts, 'What is it? What about?'

Suddenly he pulls back, his attention caught by something behind me. A rat is circling the base of the steps and Maurice reaches round in front of me to the window sill and casts about with dirty fingers for a small stone which he hurls with gusto at the animal.

'Little buggers,' he mutters, then without any warning, he steps back into the room and holds the door for me. I take a breath and follow him inside. I can almost see the air in the room: it's a kind of foul, milky stew of unwashed body and rotten food. All the curtains are drawn, and here and there, I see the stumps of yellow candles. He backs into the sitting room and perches against a table. Behind him a computer screen flickers into life.

'Where's your dog?' I say brightly.

'Dead.'

'Oh … I'm sorry.' We stare at each other.

'S'alright. I never liked him. Ate more than I did.'

'Yeah, you've … er … lost weight.'

'Have I?'

'Mmm.'

'Well. So …' he begins.

'Well.'

'What do you …? I mean I don't want to be rude but –'

'Ben,' I say.

'Ben?'

'I heard from him.'

He comes very close and puts a hand on my shoulder, looks into my eyes. 'You're kidding? That can't be …' I nod. 'You heard from him?'

'Well, I heard from a woman. I had a call from a woman who said she's seen him, been with him … that he's in China –'

'Could be made up, hoax.'

'I don't think so. No. I don't think so.'

He pulls out a chair and sits himself at the computer, his knuckles shining blue in the screen light. I notice a photograph in a plastic frame of a woman with bright red hair, blowing. She's smiling with her head on one side.

'Can't be, can't be …' he says, more to himself than me.

'Maurice? Why? Why don't you think –?'

'I looked. You wouldn't believe it. I spent months on it … best part of a year, looking for him. When I heard about it … his family, you know, the police … the appeal, the papers, I started looking. Nothing. Not a dicky bird.'

'But that doesn't mean anything. I mean … just because –'

'I've got contacts,' he mutters darkly.

'Dick? Is he still –?'

'Dick's dead. Caught this bloody thing, didn't he? Went to ground in his bunker. Died like an animal, they said, poor lad.'

'But before –?'

'I didn't see much of him after … after Ben. He was in London mostly. I know he tried to find him. Wrote about it in his blog.'

'I'm sorry,' and then I have to tell him because she's pushing at my eyes and my mouth. 'My sister died. She … caught it … she died.'

He looks up at me and nods. 'Sorry to hear that, dear.' I nod and I bite on my lip to stop the sobs that are boiling in my throat. He rummages on the table and rattles a tin under my nose and I look down at a sorry assortment of chocolate covered biscuits that mice have got to first.

'It's OK, thanks. I'm OK.'

He shrugs, picks one out, dusts off a little black missile of mouse shit, pops the biscuit into his mouth and sucks at it. 'So, Ben? You think he's alive?'

I nod. 'Yeah. Yeah I think so. I mean I know it's crazy after all this time but …'

'Mmm. Well. Anything's possible.'

'I know you've tried but I thought maybe you … we … maybe we could try again?' In my pocket is the letter I wrote to Ben and without thinking I pull it out and squeeze it tight in my fist.

'What's that you've got there?'

I unfold it, smooth it and hand it to him. 'It's nothing. It's a … a letter I wrote to Ben. When I was … never mind.'

'Want me to put it out there? Into cyber space for you? See if he bites?'

I look at him and he looks back, red rimmed eyes unblinking. I nod slowly. 'Maybe.'

'What's that mean, "maybe"? Do you want me to or not?'

'Yes. Yes. Do it. Please.'

He grunts and takes it and puts it in his pocket. 'Why me anyway? You must have chums who can do this sort of thing?'

'I don't. I mean … it's complicated. You knew Ben. I feel like an idiot. I had no idea you'd been looking for him all the time. I suppose I thought you might be able to help. You know, use your contacts on the –'

'The Grid? What d'you think I've been doing? It's not easy though. Mostly the only thing people ever talk about is cures and suchlike, you know. It's more of a forum these days really. Might be better to get on the telly.'

'I found out something about it the other day.'

He looks up and I tell him what I heard from Charlie. He doesn't look surprised.

'I know that. It's hardly flu is it? Spite of what they might want us to think. There's been talk on the web about that for a while now. Conspiracy theorists got their knickers in a twist about it. Didn't think it would be the North Koreans though … that is a turn up. Thought it might be the Iranians. You never can tell with foreigners …'

'What I wondered was … you know, if Ben was –'

'Involved?'

'Well, you know, with his Dad and everything? Rees?'

'Mmm. Rees. Yes. Yes …' He reaches into the tin for another biscuit. 'Rees are up to their bloody necks in it, I reckon.'

'You think?'

He taps away for a second or two and a grainy image flickers up: a grey-haired man in tinted glasses with a sheaf of files under his arm talking to someone who has his back to the camera. 'Little covert snap: this is the fella we think who took over at Rees – big wig scientist, doctor – they claim they've had nothing to do with it, but we're watching.' He folds his arms and a thin line of biscuit powder settles on his chest.

'Who is it?' I say.

'Don't know the name – very secretive – but like I say, he's on the watch list. Don't if he's working with the government or what, but he's still there and he's up to something.'

'Is Rees still going then? I didn't know –'

'Not as it was, obviously. But something's going on there.'

My throat's dry. My mind's buzzing. I say, 'Ben had a letter from his Dad about helping him, finishing his journey … his research. Do you think, maybe …?'

'No!' he almost shouts it. 'That's not Ben. He was … he was a great lad. He was sickened by what his Dad was up to.'

'I know, I know. But maybe someone got to him? Made him?'

'It's possible, I suppose. Where was it he went now?'

'He had this ticket for Kunming, I think it was ... I remember, I looked it up. I'd never heard of it.'

'Kunming. That's right. I even had a contact in Hong Kong went over there for me. Spoke to police, airport staff. He'd had a fake passport, remember? I asked about him in both names. Nothing. Not a sausage. No one could even confirm he'd been on the plane at all, let alone got off it. I drew a total blank everywhere I looked. To be honest, I was going to go over there myself but then this thing broke out and ... well ...'

I stare at him, and I'm thinking about how little I did, and how when he never came back, I thought it was me he was leaving, and rather than putting any effort into properly looking for him, I wasted a load of time feeling abandoned. I squeak, 'Thank you.'

'Thank you? What for? I did it for him. For me. He was my mate. I know he'd had a tough time, poor lad. I wanted to help him. You know Dick found out something ...'

'What?'

He drops his voice to a gruff whisper: 'Aconite Hydrochloride. It's what that woman found traces of in that syringe.'

'Yes. I heard. And they killed him with it.'

'Well. Maybe. Dick thought it was odd though. He looked in to it. It's used to give the appearance of death: you know, slows heart rate right down, pupils stay fixed, no pulse ...'

'I don't understand ...'

'Well … it might be … just saying … suppose someone wanted to, or you wanted to –?"

I catch up. 'Pretend to … fake your death? Shit! But he –'

'The carbon monoxide?'

I nod.

'Mmm. Well, Dick did a bit of digging around. Did you know there was a small hole cut in the garage door? Neat job it was. Cut and then filled in. Just room enough for a pipe from the exhaust …'

'You mean …?'

'Well, it's all supposition but let's just suppose you wanted out, to just disappear? What's the best way to do it?'

A choking nausea creeps over me like smoke. I nod. 'You make it look like suicide. But surely there'd have been an ambulance? Police?'

He waves a hand. 'That's easy. That's all part of the pantomime. The key thing is – did he fake it? A pipe from the exhaust pushed through a hole in the door? The Aconite Hydrochloride in his system followed by a shot of adrenaline when he's clean away … I don't know. That's what Dick told me before he died.'

'Did you tell anyone else?'

He looks at me and blinks slowly. 'D'you think anyone would believe me? I mean I'm not even sure that's what did happen but …'

I cross to a chair and sit opposite him. 'So, it's his Dad. I mean if what you say is true, then this thing –

this disease – this ... whatever it is we're all living with, the thing that killed my sister ... Ben's Dad could have made it? That make him a mass murderer.'

Maurice paws at his stubble and I hear the scratch. 'It's possible,' he says.

I stare at him in the gloom.

19

The tunnel narrows towards the end, forcing me to lie in the sour water again and push with my feet and one good elbow. Far above me I can hear the faint drum of traffic on the freeway and here in the tunnel, the constant drip of water off the bricks over my head. I have to work for every inch of tunnel and after every inch I have to stop and breathe and nurse my arm which pulses hot against the splint. Once, half way through, I black out with the pain and come to minutes later with my face in the water choking for air.

When I fall out of the mouth of the tunnel into a shallow channel of water, I'm wasted. My arm is buzzing: the pain's in my shoulder now and I feel dizzy and sick. A kind of icy heat settles in my gut. I lie on my back and let the water swell around me.

'Get up,' I tell myself. 'Move.'

And slowly, I turn, push up on my knees and haul myself away from the tunnel mouth and the stinking water and up into the city. It's dark but I have no idea what time it is. It seems like a year ago I left the fight.

Rooster was right. The freeway's behind me. I come up on a wide empty street with no pavement and no street lights. A row of lock-ups on one side covered in graffiti and above them, a shabby tower block with thick dark balconies one on top of the other. Up ahead is a small kind of shed with a corrugated roof.

A light flashes on up in the flats over the lock-ups and a shadow crosses a window. I duck out of sight against the wall and make my way carefully to the shed. It's about a metre square and when I peer in through the doorway – because there is no door – it looks like about five or six kids have had the same idea as me. Dark shapes huddle against each other but all I can see that tells me they're human is the odd bare foot poking out from the scrum. I back out and further up the street I find a broken trestle table under which I spend probably the most uncomfortable night of my life. I'm soaking wet, I smell like filth and the pain in my arm is unbelievable. And I'm sick. I know I'm sick.

When I wake up, my whole body is shaking and I'm wet with hot sweat. I curl into a crab and try to rock myself out of it but I can't stop the mad shivering. I want to eat but my stomach's boiling and there's bile in my throat. When I open my eyes, the brightness blinds me: a sharp flash of green and red and sunlight on glass and I slam my arm over my face. It's not just my body – I feel like I'm losing my mind. Like whatever fever this is has burrowed inside every thought I've ever had and now they're all rushing at me twisted and perverted: Kamala's there, and Sophy, and Mum, Dad, everyone that's ever meant anything to me – except that now they're ugly and angry at me. I lie there curled in the dirt under the broken table trying to think about nothing: about roof tiles and Coke cans and exercise books, and all the time I'm shivering. And all around me, noise is building: shouts and yells, the odd parp of a motorbike horn. Then there's a shout above the noise and then there's no noise and then lots of whispers and exclamations and I know, even though my eyes are closed and my face is covered, that it's about me.

Hands are tugging at me. I even feel a soft barefoot kick in my side. Someone touches my broken arm and I let out an animal howl that takes me by surprise. There's a hush then and I feel the circle around me widen. And then I hear them hiss at me: the word, 'fha rang' which I know means 'European'. Slowly, I open one eye and the brightness is blistering. A stinging red heat hits me straight in the retina. I can't see right: there's a kind of haze in front of everything like I'm looking through thick glass. Shapes big and small dance and buzz in front of me. I close up and lie back exhausted.

Hands under me. Wire. Canvas. Wheels. A motor like a lawnmower. I think I'm shouting, pushing. There's water but I don't know how to drink anymore. I'm burning but I can't drink. My mouth is like a dry arch. And the people in my head are crowding in on me, accusing me, cussing me. Then, new smells and peace. Peace from the raging heat, peace from the pain and the dirt, and I don't know how or why or what's happened, but whatever it is, I can rest.

Fuzzy sounds worm into my ears and form themselves into words: 'Hey. Hey. Good morning? Hello? You English? Speak English? *Sprechen sie Deutsch?*'

I turn to the source of the sound and open my eyes again. Something is moving slowly towards me, around me, a bulky shape that becomes a person – a man. Tall and broad with dark brown eyes deep in their sockets, he wears a loose robe tied at the waist.

He repeats in a soft American drawl: 'You speak English? Can you hear me?' He leans in and his breath hangs over my face in a sour fog.

I nod once. 'English.'

I go to push myself off the bed but I'm so wasted that all it takes is a hand on my chest and I'm flat on my back again. And it's then I start to sob. Like I haven't cried since I was six years old. The man slides a cold hand across my forehead. 'You're OK. You're OK. You're safe. I'm not going to hurt you.'

I sink back and it's then that I see my broken arm. It's been set in plaster up to my shoulder and I'm in clean clothes. The room's in focus now: a small neat space with a bed and two arm chairs and a bead curtain over a door to what looks like a tiny kitchen. I sniff and ask, 'Who are you?'

'I'm Aaron. From Wyoming originally but with one person per square mile out there and most of them crazy, makes you want to get out once in a while. I came to China with a friend and just kind of stayed here.'

'So how −?'

'How long have I been here? Since before all the trouble in the West. Since before being a foreigner can get you arrested. You been taking a big chance running around this city.'

'Eh?'

He raises an eyebrow and he's about to say something when a long high-pitched whistle sounds from beyond the curtain.

'Tea?'

I nod. He disappears into the kitchen from where I hear the homely clatter of cups and spoons, and when he emerges, he's holding a tray with a cup of jasmine tea and a bowl of what turns out to be hot egg noodles with chicken. He helps me sit up, places the tray across my lap, then settles back into a chair and smooths the top of his head with both hands. He's completely bald. The noodles are good and I shovel them in, lapping up the juice. He smiles contentedly. 'OK. First things first. Let's hear about you. Awesome tattoo by the way. Where d'you get it? Thailand?'

I shake my head. 'I'm Ben. I …' and then I stop cold because I have absolutely no way of even understanding what I've been through, let alone actually talking about it to another human being. I decide to lie. 'I got beaten up. Got my money nicked, passport, everything. I was coming up from Pu'er in the south. On … on a bus … I fell asleep and I –'

He nods, watching me with the chopsticks. 'How long have you been in China?'

'Too long. I just want to get home. Thank you for … you know … I didn't think I was going to last much longer.'

'Sure.'

'Thanks for … thank you.'

He's still staring. 'No problem.'

I look up at him over the bowl. 'How did you find me?'

'Market traders found you. I was just passing. You were lucky.'

'I know.'

'I mean you're lucky I came along when I did.'

'Well … yeah.'

There's a silence. 'You don't know, do you?'

'What?'

'Where the fuck have you been, man?'

'Sorry. I don't get it –'

'Sure you do.' There's a slight change in his tone. And he gets up and crosses the room and switches on the light. The bulb swings between us casting shadows on the walls.

I put down the bowl and I say again, 'What are you talking about?'

He lets out a breath, sits back down. 'You really don't know? You been living in a cave or something?'

'You mean the ... the flu thing – the sickness?'

'Yes,' he says slowly. 'Let's start with that.'

'I know about it. A bit. But I've been –'

'Yeah. Yeah, you said.'

'So. Tell me.'

'OK. My brother and his girlfriend live in Manhattan. He's an accountant, or at least he was. They haven't left their apartment block in two months. Every week, a food truck comes by and they put a rope down and haul up what's left. Not that there is much because of the looting in the tunnels and on the bridges, and the freight embargos. The streets are full of garbage, there's not enough water and people are going crazy. I mean really crazy. I guess London's the same. Five hundred thousand people have died in Manhattan alone since this started: rich, poor, old, young. And you know what? You catch this thing and you're usually dead in a week. What I heard, first you go crazy then your body just ... it just kind of blows up. But you want to know the worst of it? There's no cure. They've hit it with everything they've got and they're no closer.'

Is this him, what he made? Can it be?

A slow twisting like a rope being turned inside of me. I can see him: his face through the mask, through the bio hazard suit, hear the squeak of plastic, the gurgle of his breathing through the tubes on his back.

But I say, 'Can they leave? Your brother?'

'Leave? Ha! Yeah, sure. Why didn't they think of that? Are you kidding? What d'you think was the first thing the authorities did? Even way before most of us knew what was going on? They shut the place down. New York, London, they're locked down. No one comes in or out. They're growing cabbages in Central Park.'

'Fuck,' I breathe.

'Yeah. That's what they're so scared of here. Months ago, when this thing blew up they gave us a week to leave the country. Everyone, well or sick, all foreign nationals had to go. That's why they were so agitated when they found you. Because: a, you were sick, and b, you're a foreigner, and c – never mind c – I had to pay them off to get you.'

'You didn't think I was sick then?'

He goes to the narrow window. 'I know the signs. And I …' he swallows. 'You'd have probably been dead by now anyway. You know you've been here three days?'

I shake my head in disbelief.

'You just had a fever. It was your arm that was infected. I gave you antibiotics and it's all OK.'

'I have to get home.'

He nods. 'I know. I know you do.'

'So what can I …? Where can I …? Do you have a computer? Laptop I can use?'

He stares at me. 'I … No. I don't. Too dangerous. I use the internet cafés.'

'Sure, I didn't think.'

'So you're heading home? Back to England?'

I nod.

'And you want to know if you can just go to the airport and get on a plane to Heathrow?'

I stare at him. 'I thought you said … That's what they want isn't it? To send people home?'

'Well … Once that was what they wanted. And that is what they did. Once. I would say there's maybe a handful of foreigners still living in China now. The programme was pretty rigid, they got to everyone: mission workers in little rural communities, bankers in Shanghai. It's just that now there really are no planes. Because there's nowhere to take you. UK and US airspace is pretty much closed.'

'So what will they do with me?'

'Well … they'll say that they're going to quarantine you for ten days, and that you'll be given a ticket out of there but the truth, I'm afraid, is a little different than that.'

'Go on.'

'I only know this because it almost happened to me.'

He leaves the window and sits back down opposite me. 'I was one of the last to go. I was one of a group from this area in the first few weeks after the epidemic. I was living the other side of the city and they tracked me down. Someone in my building informed on me. They took us – about twenty of us – and we all ended up in this disused factory shed across town. And we waited, and we waited. There were men, women and

kids. None of us had wanted to go. We all had …
connections here. So there we all were –'

There's a strange cry from down below and he
crosses again to the window, tweaks the blind, and turns
back to me. 'Nothing. Where was I? We were all there,
waiting to be – I don't know – rescued, put on a plane,
a boat, whatever … when someone got sick and then
we all got sick. And that was that.'

'You had it? You got sick?'

'I said I got sick, I didn't say I had the sickness. I
figured it out pretty soon. They were poisoning us. The
food they were giving us. Some of the people died.
That was the plan all along. There were no planes or
boats. There were never going to be. The only place
we were going was head down into a very deep hole.
And then all they got to say is: "They got sick. They
died. We buried them."'

'Jesus. What did you do?'

'I stopped eating. I tried to persuade the others to
do the same. I guess I knew they were never going to
let us go. I think I knew right from the get-go. I saw
it in their eyes. They were scared. Everybody's scared.
A few of us made it out, helped the others, for some
it was too late. I lived in caves in the mountains for a
while but I came back to the city and I've been here
ever since. I dress as a monk. I go out for food to the
market once a day and I wear my hood, my …robes.
I speak the local dialect. Nobody hassles me. Nobody
even looks at me. Worst of it is: some say it's our own

governments – our own countries – don't want us back, that it's them behind this latest operation.'

'Why … why are you still here though?'

Just then there's a rap at the door. I look at him but he's calm. Two further raps, then a soft click of a key being turned and into the room walks a young Chinese woman with cropped hair. She goes to him and they kiss and then they both turn to look at me.

'You're awake,' she says. I nod slowly. 'Hi! We met before but you were out. I'm Poppy.'

'Ben. Hi.'

She puts out a tiny hand and I shake it. Aaron says, 'I was just going to tell Ben about how come I'm still in China and then the reason turns up in person. You OK?'

She nods quickly and disappears through the curtain for a moment before coming out with three bottles of beer. 'So what are we going to do with him?' she says.

'I want to get home. I need to get home.'

'Sure.' She looks at Aaron with anxious eyes. 'It is him isn't it?'

He shoots her a look and a slight shake of the head.

'What?' I say.

'Nothing,' she says brightly. 'So … D'you think Henry could …?' she says to Aaron.

He nods. 'Just what I was thinking.'

20

The following night is hot and wet: insects spin round and round the light bulb – fat moths and mosquitoes – and from the street all I can hear is the empty whining of dogs. It's a quarter past midnight when I hear footsteps on the stairs. We've been sitting, waiting, with nothing to say because there is nothing to say. The silence is a part of it all: the waiting. I'm impatient to go but scared shitless of what's out there.

I gave them all the money I had from Yun.

My arm's feeling better and I feel better. Stronger. Earlier in the day, I stood in front of the bathroom mirror and looked at myself. My skin's pale and bitten and bruised and I look old, but under the skin I think I'm still what they made me: a fighter.

After the footsteps, there's a tapping on the door and Poppy looks at Aaron who's been sitting watching at the window. He nods, and she gets to her feet and pulls back the bolts. A vast mountain of a man is standing on the threshold.

'This is Henry,' she says.

He steps just into the room but no further. He fills the space and dwarfs the three of us. He's Thai, I think. Every inch of his flesh is thick with tattoos that weave in and out of each other: great fish, elephants, naked women, swim and stride and stretch themselves across his skin.

He nods to me and says, 'So, this is him?'

Aaron says, 'He's ready.'

He looks me over. 'You fit? You OK? You need to be strong.'

I nod but I look at Aaron for more.

He says, 'Henry's going to get you across the border into Vietnam. He knows a guy has a plane can get you to the border. The Vietnamese aren't quite so careful about foreign nationals as long as you got money.'

'Vietnam? But that's like –'

'It'll take about a day. Start now, you'll be at Hekou on the border in time to get across. It's closed from 5.00 pm every day.'

'The money I gave you – is it enough? I don't have any more but I –'

'All taken care of.'

I look from one to the other. 'But … I don't understand. Why would you –?'

'Do we need a reason?'

'No, but …'

'You're a fellow traveller in life – it's good karma to help someone … and you'll maybe pay it on someday.'

'Thank you. Thanks guys. Thanks so much. When I get home I can –'

'No you can't. Believe me. If it's anything like the States, a lot will have changed.'

Henry grunts and goes out and I turn on the threshold. Poppy gives me a hug and Aaron shakes my hand. He looks over my shoulder to where Henry's waiting, leans toward me and says softly, 'I recognised you at once.'

'Eh?'

'From the picture,' he says.

I hear Henry's keys jangle behind me.

'Sorry. What picture?'

'The pictures – of you.'

I stare at him and he goes on: 'Like a wanted poster – your face – all over the city – on TV. Someone's looking for you. You seriously didn't know?'

'Fuck. Ping's people … they must have –'

'Ping?'

'Just … no one. Thanks. Thanks for telling me.'

'Sure. It's just that … there's a reward, see? So …'

'A reward?'

'Just that. And a number to call.'

A cold sick feeling starts up in my gut. 'Aaron,' I say, 'did you … I mean …. Have you …?'

He's shaking his head. 'I wouldn't do that. I swear. I didn't. I wouldn't.'

I'm sweating now. 'And him? Henry? He knows doesn't he? He fucking knows.'

He puts a hand on my shoulder. 'Just trust me, OK? I told you, Henry will take care of you.'

I can hear him behind me. 'I don't have a choice,' I say.

I follow Henry. Aaron's given me a pair of camouflage trousers and a dark T shirt which looks like it might have belonged to someone of Henry's size. He hands me a woollen hat which I pull down hard. I hurry after him down the stairs and out into the night where an ex-army jeep is waiting.

Henry turns to face me outside. The night heaves around us.

'You thirsty?' he growls.

'I … I guess …' I say.

He goes to the cabin and rummages around and returns with a bottle. 'Drink it. I'm not stopping. Drink it now. Piss in it later. Understand?'

I nod and drink. He helps me into the back of the jeep, leans in and pulls at a thin cord in the floor. A door wings opens and I see there's a cavity the size of a coffin: just enough room for me to lie flat inside it. With Henry's help, I climb in and lie down, tucking my arm across my chest. On either side of the cavity are two wooden slits like gills to breathe. I lie back and breathe hard as he slots the door back into place and I hear him wheezing as he works to pile things on top of me.

I feel everything in that box. I feel Henry shift his weight in his seat, I feel him changing gears, pumping the pedals; but more than that, I feel every rut and every stone on every road we pass. After about twenty minutes of twisting and turning and braking and accelerating, we swing out onto what feels like smooth tarmac and he picks up the speed. And without meaning to, because I've never been more jumpy, I fall asleep to the rattle of the engine and the road running underneath us.

I wake up as the jeep judders to a halt. It's freezing in the box and every pore prickles with cold. I move my toes and fingers which is pretty much all I can move, and I wait, listening to my breathing. The air is stale.

There are voices and the sound of heavy boots. The door opens and slams shut and I hear Henry, his voice raised, sounding indignant and snappy, speaking in dialect at a machine gun pace. Other voices – two I think – are at the back of the jeep now. I can hear the grit crunch under their soles. Someone opens the doors. I freeze like a snake, I slow my breathing and swallow salt. Some shouting then, and things are being moved and pushed above me. And I think I could die here. I can die here. A bullet in the head - a moment of choking fear then the sting of the metal in my skull and nothing: dust and teeth left in some shallow grave years from now.

I ready myself. A thin beam of light from a torch through the crack where the lid fits the cavity and I'm perfectly still. Two minutes later, a torch is shining in my eyes and a rough hand is pulling me out of my hiding place. At once I look for Henry. He's standing a little way off under a street lamp smoking a cigarette, and the thin fumes curl up from his mouth towards the light where the moths are dancing. I catch his eye and he looks right back at me, lifts his shoulders in a heavy shrug, stubs out his cigarette and turns away.

There are two guys in the truck with me now. They're both masked and armed with sub-machine guns and they're wearing some kind of military or police uniform. I follow them down and look around me. I guess I'd thought we'd be in some random lay-by off the freeway but we're not at all. We're in a kind of large fenced enclosure with a series of single-storey buildings like army barracks, all joined to each other at angles like dominos across the ground. There are other vehicles parked up in the distance, and a long way off, a single engine aircraft. One of the men gestures to me to walk and we track across stubby grass towards one of the long huts. There's no sign of Henry any more. And you know, I'm not even angry with him. It's the way the world is, I've decided. Why shouldn't he sell me out? I'm nothing to him. The only thing that freaks me out is that Aaron and Poppy had something to do with it, and if they didn't, what's going to happen to them if they're found out.

But these people don't look like they work for Ping.

It's dim inside the hut. The only light comes from a desk lamp in an office near the door. A thin Chinese man with square glasses, wearing a grubby mask, sits over a pile of paperwork. Poking out from a sheaf of files, I catch a glimpse of what looks like a British passport. He gets up when I come in and calls me over. That's when the guys from the truck leave me. One of them says something but I don't catch it. I see them through the window walking away, talking animatedly, their brass and buttons winking in the lights.

The man looks me up and down, gestures to me to sit and he sits back down across the desk from me.

'What's your name?' he says in a clipped English accent.

'Where is this?' I snap back.

'At the risk of kicking things off with a cliché, do please let me ask the questions. What is your name?'

'Ben Collins.'

'Do you have proof? A passport?'

'I don't have one.'

He looks at me sideways on. 'No,' he says.

'It … I … I was robbed.'

'That is unfortunate.'

'Where is this?'

He tuts and shakes his head at me and after a long wait, I get what I wanted. Kind of: 'Never mind where you are. That's not important.'

'I just want to get home. Back to the UK.'

'Why didn't you report to the authorities when we asked? When everyone else did?'

'I didn't know … I couldn't … I …'

'Mmm. Yes. We see a great deal of people like you, Ben Collins, people who just couldn't … wouldn't …

who think they can just work the system their way. Henry works for us, you see. We know all about Aaron. Very sweet man. He rather naively thinks his paltry little offerings are enough to buy someone like Henry, but it's a tough world we live in, Mr Collins, especially now, as I'm sure you're aware. And in your *particular* circumstances …'

He pulls out a sheet of paper torn at the corners and waves it at me. It's a crude kind of poster, and there, looking back at me, is my face: an old photo – I'm squinting into the camera. It looks like it's been badly cropped, someone's shoulder is just in shot to my right. Charlie. My father must have taken it. There's writing in Mandarin at the bottom and a number.

He shakes his head and tucks it back under the papers on his desk. I look at him. His eyes behind the glasses are grey and narrow and his forehead is high and domed. He looks like one of those tiny flesh-eating dinosaurs. Most of the time, he holds his hands out of sight behind his back and leans over the desk, his stringy neck extended, but every now and again he coughs and brings a grey fist up to his mouth under the mask. I think about what Aaron said about the quarantine station and what they did to the people waiting to leave.

'What do you want with me? Is this about fighting? About the cages? Because if –'

'*Cages*? No. It's … we need to –' Again the cough, and then he seems to change his mind. 'First things first,

we need to check your health – your arm ... your ...
I'll take you to the clinic now. And after that, we'll find
you a bed for the night.'

He stands up and begins to tap and order his papers.
I breathe out. 'Look, I'm not sick and I'm not tired. I'm
asking you just to tell me why I'm on that poster and
what you think is going to happen next.'

'What I think is going to happen next ... an
interesting way of putting it. You're not afraid of me,
are you?' I shake my head and sit back in my chair.

'I see. Yes, you're coping with ... uncertainty very
well, I can see. You've been in situations before where
things have been – shall we say – beyond your control?'

I nod once. He gets to his feet. 'Come with me
please. We'll get your arm seen to first.'

I follow him out of the office and to the end of the
hut. We pass odd pieces of office furniture stacked in
groups against the walls: filing cabinets, desk drawers
and chairs, some with missing legs, are heaped together.
At the end of the hut, we go through a door and turn
right into a corridor; then through double doors into
the clinic. In contrast to the other hut, it's light and
warm and open with plastic chairs against the walls.
There's a TV on but silent in a corner and a large table
at the end. On either side, there are curtained cubicles
and a low hum of voices echoes around us.

One of the cubicles is only half-screened and I see
a woman sitting on the bed holding a dish. Her face
is grey and every so often she retches up a stream of

bile into the dish. A nurse – at least I guess it's a nurse – stands behind her, his arms folded like he's waiting for a train, except, when he catches me looking, he crosses to the curtain and snaps it shut. An icy sweat breaks on my neck. The man I followed gestures to me to sit, and I'm thinking about how I'm going to get out of there and back on the road, and how I'll walk across the fucking continent if I have to, when I see something that stuns me so completely, I nearly break the chair I'm sitting in.

A few feet away from me, CNN is spooling on the TV and I'm half watching – seeing helicopter pictures flashing up of cities that don't look like cities any more: giant wastelands, deserted streets, weeds pushing up through paving stones, army trucks delivering water; a dead dog – its eyes swollen and glassy. And high on the tops of skyscrapers, towers, on suspension bridges, clinging like crickets, crooked bodies, their faces frozen and their eyes white.

And that's when I see her – the screen cuts to an anchor, goes blank for a second then there's a grey screen and a person in front of it talking to a hand-held camera: red hair down her back, her face pale and drawn; there's no sound, so I don't know what she's saying but then after a minute, the camera shifts and slips and when it rights itself, she's holding up a picture of me, the one she took before I left her: I'm smiling, dizzy with what just happened and my hair all sticking up. Then it cuts out and the anchor takes over and I'm pole-axed, trying to breathe with my head between my knees, and my body shaking.

'Are you OK? Ben? Mr Collins?'

He sounds far away but I'm further. I look up at him blankly but I can't speak. My voice has kind of collapsed in on itself. He tries again. 'Ben? Can you hear me?' He drops to his knees in front of me and flicks a stethoscope up at my chest. There's a nurse standing next to him – a man in a short white coat and army trousers. He nods and between them they hustle me to a cubicle where they lay me down and take some blood from my good arm.

The man is saying something, he's almost shouting, but I can't focus my eyes or ears. I'm spinning away from everyone on the planet. I'm in orbit around the earth and I can't get back. A fierce chill creeps through me and I have to fight to breathe.

It's like before. I know. All I have to do is run.

They leave me in the cubicle and I can hear them outside: a whispered conversation I don't understand. The clock on the wall opposite ratchets onto the next minute. I hear footsteps – someone else has joined them. I get to my feet and go to the curtain. The first man and the nurse stand with their backs to me. They're listening to another man. He's short and stout, and his face is lined and spotted with little black warts and moles and I know him at once: Dr Yeo from my father's clinic in the camp.

I run then. I bulldoze through the little group at full tilt and send them flying. And as I run, I pull back whatever I can find – chairs, desk lamps – to block their way. The door at the end opens easily and I turn and fly through the first hut and headlong through the doors into the night.

A guard runs at me but I throw up my plaster cast, catch him in the jaw and follow with a shin kick to his groin. He staggers back shouting and there's another one after him. He's shorter than me and I elbow him in the head and send him down. I back into the shadow of another hut and wait catching my breath. I've cracked the cast and my arm is agony. I clutch it into myself and ready myself to run, when there's a gentle hand on my shoulder and a voice whispers my name: 'Ben. They told me. It is you?' I turn and it's him –Yeo – looking up at me in the half light from the hut, his eyes pinched into a smile. I'm breathing hard. 'I've been looking for you.' There's something about the way he's talking that pulls me back from where I'm going and holds me there. I nod.

'Please, come inside.' The soft touch on my arm, the friendly nod. 'Come. No one is going to hurt you. Please?'

I don't know where we go but we end up in a small blank room with two chairs and a low table: he sits me down and faces me. 'Your cast is … we can reset it, don't worry.' He puts the tips of his fingers together and taps them over and over. 'I expect you want to get home? To England, yes?'

I look at him. I lean towards him, ignoring the pain in my arm, and I swallow and will the words: 'What are you doing here?'

'Ben, I'll tell you everything. Just come with me.'

'Why should I trust you?'

'Mmm?'

'Why. Should. I. trust. You?'

'Well. That is a good question.' He puts his head on one side. 'I think that, here and now we don't need to worry about trust – trusting each other. The world is very crazy right now. Maybe is just good to have a bit of what we want, maybe that is perhaps enough? For now, at least?'

'You're not going to poison me – not like the rest of them,' I say.

The tapping stops. 'Where did you hear that?'

'Never mind. It's true, isn't it?'

He blinks and rubs his eyes. 'I know nothing about that. People had a chance to go – to leave. Some decided not to. They were … outside the law … and when you do that, then bad things can happen. It's very simple.'

'You're not doing that with me.' I'm on my feet now.

'Ben, please sit down. Nobody is going to hurt you. Why on earth would I have worked so hard to find you, just to get rid of you? The posters I printed, advertisements in newspapers … you must know what I'm talking about?'

I stare at him and sit down slowly. He goes on: 'Oh. I thought I was … you know about the sickness? In the West?'

'A little.'

'You know it's not just a … an ordinary virus? You must have thought … suspected … surely … *this is it*: the viral/fungal hybrid that your father was making for Rees.'

I stare at him. I was right. 'But he –' I start, but I know the truth before he tells it.

'He stopped work on it, I know,' he says. 'He even tried to destroy what he'd done. But the … the damage was done. They finished it, they sold it: to a terrorist group out of North Korea, and they set about using it in cities in the West. Hundreds of thousands of people have died and many more will across the globe. It's in the UK, the US. It's already crossed into mainland Europe. It's just a matter of time before –'

'But the vaccine, he made a vaccine. I was –' I say.

'Yes. Yes, he did, and as you know – of course you know – it took a long time. This hybrid is very, very difficult to measure, to contain. It grows very rapidly and, of course, it has the fungal element which is so very deadly.'

'But it's there isn't it? The vaccine? He said it was done. I don't understand.'

'He made it, yes. But it was hopeless. There was no time to communicate what he had done – the formula – to the right people. And he was so security conscious, you see. He wanted sole responsibility. You know – the attack on the camp – it was going to fall into the wrong hands, the whole project, and before they could get at it, he destroyed it – every drop, every ounce. He had no choice. All his work. He got you out just in time. You're the only hope right now, Ben.'

'So, why did he … why didn't he stay alive for fuck's sake? Why did he just –' But I can't finish. I don't know if I'll ever be able to say it out loud.

'He did what he did because he wasn't prepared to be used any more by anyone, do you see?'

'But he's just made things worse.'

He leans back. 'Not necessarily. They don't have a vaccine which makes them more careful about how they use the weapon, and we … we have you.'

'So how did you get out?'

He fixes me with blank eyes. 'I disguised myself as a prisoner.'

'But you worked on it too, you must know how to –'

'He let no one in – not completely. He trusted no one.'

'So there's no vaccine in the West?'

'They're trying to understand it – trying to work on it – scientists in the US and the UK – but the virus is resistant – intelligent. It's very, very difficult to contain and understand. Rees were close but they didn't quite get there.'

'And now?'

'And now,' he looks up at me. 'We have you. I have you. And we have hope. You have the vaccine in you. You're what everyone will be looking for – the missing link, if you like – they just don't know it yet. But when they do, they will come looking for you. And that's why I'm going to get you out, get you home.'

He leans in and whispers, 'Your blood is so precious. That's why I've been looking for you for so long. When this happened, I knew I had to find you. I went through the records and flight details for every westerner who left mainland China after you got out, and I concluded you must still be here.'

'Whatever.' My head is still hanging between my knees and I can feel the blood humming in my ears.

'Are you ready?'

'What?'

'I'm telling you, you can go home. I can make this happen. I can get clearance for you to leave as soon as you're ready. We'll fix up your arm and we can go. We will have a plane waiting. Would you like to use the telephone? To ... to call your family?'

I look up. 'Yes. Yes, please.'

He shifts in his chair. 'Ben, there is a condition to this. We've talked about ... helping each other and I must ask you this before we go any further.'

'What?'

'I'd rather you said nothing about my involvement at the camp. Nothing about the fact that I was there. You understand?' I nod. 'I mean, my part in it all was fairly minimal, and I ... well ... ethically, I had my reservations about some of the ... I mean, I understand that he did what he did for –'

'OK. I won't say anything.' The sight of him squirming in front of me is too much to bear. 'Just give me the phone.'

21

Sophy

It's weird. All I was worried about was what to wear.
And I think about all the people who go on the telly to
appeal about missing or murdered relatives and do they
ever stop to think I'm not going to wear that because it
makes me look fat or doesn't go with my hair? Probably
not. Probably never. I'm about as shallow as they come,
but then I guess I thought about it because if he saw
it, saw me, I just wanted him to think I looked OK. So
thinking about it, there's shallow, and shallow, and then
just plain stupid, because the likelihood of him seeing
me is probably about a billion to one.

Maurice organized it though someone called
Angel. Maurice calls him a "cyber-buddy". He was a
TV producer, he made documentaries before all this
started but he's got contacts at CNN, and we did a
piece at Maurice's – rigged up a sort of screen behind

me – and they managed to get it in. It was his idea, the photograph, I would never have thought of it.

Anyway, it's all thanks to Maurice it went ahead, and I've asked him over for dinner to thank him because he looks like it's a while since he had a proper meal. Not that there's much I can offer but when it all started Dad bulk bought pasta and hid it all around the house and garden – some of it they found, but some stayed hidden. It's nearly all gone now but I'm going to make a sauce with wild mushrooms and garlic and spoil him a bit for the evening.

The shotgun is on the kitchen table. It shines in the candlelight.

He turns up half an hour early, wearing a blue balaclava and a heavy scarf that smells of dog,

'Not taking any chances,' he says, as he wipes his feet on the mat.

'Hey,' I say, 'come in.'

He stands in the middle of the kitchen and unwinds his scarf and in minutes the whole house smells of him. There's an uncomfortable moment when he emerges from the woollen hat and we look at each other. I see him look at the gun and give a slight nod of approval.

'Thanks for coming,' I say.

'You invited me,' he says, confused.

'Er … yes. Would you like something to drink?'

'Water please. Is it boiled?'

'Bottled and boiled.'

'Good-oh. That'll do me. Nice house.'

'Thanks.'

'Where's your mum and dad?'

'They've … they're away.'

He looks at me blankly. 'Away?'

'Mmm.'

I root in bare cupboards for a cup. And he doesn't let it drop. 'After your sister … going away? Seems a bit odd.'

I turn to look at him. 'The … Reapers have got them.'

'Ah.'

'They came for them. At the hospital. I guess they didn't know about me, or couldn't get to me.'

There's quiet then, and he paces round the kitchen in a circle, nodding, and then comes to a stop facing me and the look in his eyes is so soft and so fond, that I almost hug him. I feel the tears prickle behind my eyes. I turn and busy myself chopping garlic. 'This stuff, it's so tough … It's nice once it's cooked …' I say.

'It's a treat for me. Maurice loves a bit of garlic,' he says, and he pats my head so lightly and so gently that all I feel is a thin breath of air that lifts my hair and settles it again. I choke on tears. 'Thanks. Thanks.'

'You did well on the telly I think, didn't you?'

'You think? You think he'll see it?'

'I don't know, my love. I think we got to prepare ourselves for the fact that it might be a bit unlikely … but you never know. You never know.'

I nod breathing back sobs.

'Shall I set the table?' he says.

'I … I just thought we could eat in the kitchen?'

'Good plan. Where's the bits?'

'I've got two forks left and a penknife. Sorry. I was … we were burgled.'

'Oh I see … buggers aren't they? Nature of the beast, I suppose. So no silver service then?'

'I'm afraid not, Maurice.' And I manage a smile.

The minute the pasta is on the plate, he's tucking in, working his fork, spooling up the strands. He pauses mid forkful and looks up and smiles. 'Yum yum,' he says. And I can't help it he just makes me laugh.

'Sorry.'

'S'alright. I expect my table manners aren't much to write home about. Since old doggy died, I've been on my own.'

'I wasn't laughing at … God, it's ridiculous. I don't know why I was laughing. You just make me feel … better I suppose.'

He ducks to the plate again and slurps up another mouthful. 'Maurice?' he looks up. 'What do you know about them – The Reapers?'

He wipes his mouth on his arm and little bits of mushroom slide off and cling to him. 'The Reapers are basically a bunch of heavies – thugs. They pretend like they're sort of leading the charge of the light brigade against this thing but they're just a load of bullies taking stuff out on other people who are just as frightened and ignorant as they are.'

'So what do they do? I mean to people they …

you know ... take?'

'You mean like your folks?'

'Yeah.'

'I don't know, my love. I really don't know. They're scared, you know. Scared people, panicked people, do funny things.'

I know he's lying. I close my eyes and feel a hand on my arm. 'You know what though? You know what I think? I think your parents will come through. I'm a great believer that good things happen to good people, and you're a good person, Sophy.'

'Thanks Maurice. You didn't see the sign on our garage door then?'

There's a pause while he twists his fork. 'Yeah. Yes. I did see that, yes.'

He leans over and picks up the shotgun. 'You know how to use this?'

'My dad showed me. It's not difficult.'

He checks the barrel and the sight. 'It is straightforward. I suppose what I really mean is, *could* you use it? On someone?'

And the answer comes to me at once. 'Yes. I could.'

He looks at me hard for a second and then he nods, satisfied. And then there's a banging at the door.

'Might be your chance,' he says snuffing the candle.

He's behind me breathing garlic as I edge to the door. The dark shape behind the glass raises a hand and Maurice whispers, 'I'll open it. You point that thing at him.'

He heaves a heavy chair away from the front door and unbolts it slowly. My palms sweat into the metal and I hitch the gun to my shoulder to steady it.

There on the doorstep is Josh, a plucked chicken hanging from his hand. He puts his hands up in mock terror and I slowly lower the weapon.

'Sorry I scared you. Where did you get the gun?' and then he stops because Maurice emerges from the shadows. 'Who's this?'

Maurice looks from Josh to me and back again, puzzled. 'I'm Maurice. I'm an old friend of Ben's. And Sophy's. Ben and Sophy's friend,' he says pointedly, so we all know exactly what he means.

'Right,' says Josh. But Maurice waits setting himself between Josh and me. Josh gives me a questioning look and I say, 'It's OK Maurice. Josh is a friend. He's been great. He's OK. Really.'

'Alright, alright…' Maurice shuffles aside and I follow Josh into the kitchen.

'What the fuck?' he whispers at me, still holding the chicken. 'Who is that guy? What are you doing here with him?'

'He's a friend. I told you. He's been helping me.'

'Helping you? Helping you do what? He's weird. He smells like –'

I never get to hear what Maurice smells like because I know he's standing behind us in the dark. He says to Josh, 'Nice chicken,' and to me, 'Your phone's ringing.'

I run. Up the stairs and across the landing to my room. The phone gives a faint blue glow. 'Hello?'

And when I hear his voice, I fall onto my knees in the dark room. 'Ben!'

22

It rings forever and I'm about to give up when there's a click as it's connected, a long echoing silence and then her voice: breathless, like she's been running and I have to swallow twice before I can speak because she's so close and so fucking far away all at the same time.

'I … Hello? *Sophy*? Is that you?'

A long, long pause and the voice comes back with my name in a gasp. And then I don't know what to say because anything and everything on the phone sounds so bland, so everyday. And I'm thinking all of that and how useless it all is and how much there is to say to her and how completely mad my life has been in the time since I last saw her, and about her and what she means to me and, yes, about Kamala and what we did and what I wanted to do, and my head is spinning but all I say is: 'Are you OK?' She's crying. I can hear her trying to breathe and suddenly it's so real.

I'm crying too. 'Sophy?'

'Ben, I can't believe it! I can't believe it! You're alive, you're OK. When she called me, the Chinese girl, after all that – I thought ...'

And I say it again because all I can think about is the sickness. I can hear Yeo moving about in the next room, a low muttering.

'Are you OK?' I say again. 'Are you ... are you sick? Just tell me you don't have –'

There's a pause and I don't know whether it's the phone or her and then she says quietly, 'My ... Lily ... my sister had it ...'

'No. Oh fuck, Sophy ... But she's –'

'Dead. Ben, everybody dies. What I wanted to know ... was it ... is this something to do with your –?'

I swallow. 'My Dad,' I finish her sentence. 'Yeah. This is him – *was* him – but it's not what you think. He changed, he tried to make amends. He –' And she cuts me off because she's crying again: short breaths and heavy sobs. 'Sophy, listen – I'm sorry. I'm so sorry. I'm sorry about Lily, about everything. I had no idea. I've been out of contact; I didn't know about any of this. Listen, I'm coming home. I'm going to –' Still I'm talking to her tears, and then suddenly I hear a tap and movement and a man's voice on the end of the phone.

'Who is this?' he's saying.

'Who are *you*? Put Sophy back on,' I say. I can hear her in the background.

'She's too upset. Maybe she'll call you later when she's feeling better.'

'PUT HER BACK ON!'

'Hey. Buddy. No need to shout – I'm just trying to help. Who is this?'

'Who the fuck are you?' My hand's squeezing the receiver, pushing it against my head. And then he goes and says, 'I'm a friend of Sophy's,' and there's something in the way he says it that makes me think he's missing out the 'boy' part. And I guess he means me to get that. I would in his place.

'A friend,' I say. 'Right. A friend …'

'That's right, mate.'

'I'm not your mate.'

'Just take it easy,' he says.

'Just let me talk to her.'

'She doesn't want to talk to you.'

I hear her then: 'Josh. It's OK. Give me the phone'

I hear a whispered altercation, footsteps, then her voice again. Choked. I can feel myself losing it.

'Ben,' she whispers.

'Was that … Are you …?' I can't get the words out.

'He's a friend.' And I wait, and it's like looking down a long railway tunnel for a train you know is going to run you over and you can't do a thing about it, when she says, even though she doesn't have to and she doesn't owe me anything: 'He's just a friend. He's in the army.'

'The army?'

'Yeah. They're everywhere. Keeping areas quarantined, bringing in food trucks and stuff …'

'Christ.'

'You said you're coming home? When? *How*? They've closed the airspace.'

'Someone's organizing it. It's a big deal in a way … because of who I am … what I am. I –'

Yeo is behind me now. 'Enough,' he says.

I nod but Sophy's saying, 'You mean your Dad? What, have they've arrested you or –?'

'No. It's not that … I … it's that … well … I think I can cure this … this sickness … I can –'

And before I know it, a crooked finger has stabbed at the phone and cut me off. He wags it at me and says, 'I said, *enough*. We are ready to fix your arm now.'

My head's spinning. I stare at him.

In the next room, a trolley and a nurse are waiting.

'Take off your shirt, Ben,' says Yeo, and the nurse steps forward to help me. 'Turn around for a moment … Ah, I remember this,' he says and whisks a palm over my back. 'Snake. Good symbol. Your father chose this for you. It is very special.'

'Whatever.'

'It remind you of your father, I suppose?'

I fold the shirt with my good hand. 'I don't know. It reminds me of what I am – of what he made me.'

'No, no. It's special. Very good.'

'You get one if you like it so much.'

He coughs and mutters something under his breath. The nurse motions me to sit back and rest my arm on the counter and takes a full syringe from a metal tray.

'What's that?'

Yeo smiles and nods at the nurse. 'To numb the pain.
We're going to have to break it to reset it. We can put
you out if you wish but I'd rather we didn't have to'

'No. Just do it,' I say, and I brace myself as the needle
goes in. Soon I'm floating and there's no pain: I can hear
the crunch and grind of bone on bone, the wet slap
of the plaster cast being reapplied. I close my eyes and
I see Sophy, except that now all I see is some soldier
with his arm around her, comforting her because I've
just told her I as good as killed her sister. And what
makes it worse – and what makes me doubt myself for
ever wanting to get back in the first place – is that I've
done exactly the same over here. I met someone and
found myself wanting more. What's to stop her doing
the same?

I doze in and out of consciousness and wake up
with Yeo's fingers tapping and pulsing at my back, and
my arm set in plaster and bound in a sling. He seems
twitchy.

'Time to go,' he says, and helps me on with my shirt.
Dawn's breaking as we leave: a pale red glow licking at
the horizon. He hustles me to a waiting jeep and gives
me a blanket. 'Put this over you.'

I take it from him. 'Why?'

I catch a flicker in his eyes. 'You must not be seen.'

'What's going on? Is this OK, what you're doing
here? I thought you said you had clearance?'

'Ben. It's OK,' he says. 'We had an arrangement. It's
all fine. We have a plane waiting across the border.'

'Why should I trust you?'

'I thought we talked about trust. It's not necessary here and now. Just get in the jeep. Everything's ready. Just do as you're told, please.'

A light goes on in a nearby hut and he pushes and pulls me into the jeep, rams it into gear and races towards the exit. There's no one at the gates and he drives full pelt at them; in the back seat I feel them buckle and snap under us. The wheels spin out onto the highway and I peer out to see them sending up smoke from the tarmac into the morning mist.

We slow for what must be the border traffic and I lie down dead still in the back under the blanket, listening to a thousand voices and my own breathing, hot and thick.

Finally, I hear Yeo shout something. The engine picks up and we rumble on, and after a while, I fall asleep. I dream about Sophy: she's behind us on the road out of China, she's calling to me but her dress is a tight Chinese silk and wraps her to her ankles and she can't run, she can't move and I can't stop moving. I see her red hair and the blue silk dress, and I'm moving further away until she's out of sight and all I hear is the faint echo of my name being called.

And then it is being called: it's Yeo, tugging at the blanket. The sun's high overhead and there's the sound of crickets singing in the trees around us. For a moment, the white brightness of it all burns the back of my eyes and I have to blink to get used to it.

'Where are we?'

He twists in his seat and points, and a hundred yards away from us, in a field, with the sunlight flashing and dancing on its metal casing, sits a silver twin-prop aeroplane. I stare at him.

'Transport,' he says simply. 'This will get you home. The pilot will take us. We stop in Mumbai, then in Istanbul, to refuel.'

I climb out and sink – I sit right down in the middle of the road and shove my head under my good arm, and all I can see is a tiny square of charcoal coloured grit under me, sharp little angles stuck fast forever.

'Ben?'

I can feel his hand on me but I can't look up at him. 'Can I … my blood … can you do this – make this – without him?' I say.

But all he says is, 'Ben, it's time to go. We need the light.'

Slowly, I haul myself off the ground and follow him to the waiting plane.

The pilot, a tall man with a wiry moustache who calls himself Jim, greets us. I look back once before I climb aboard, and once again as we pull skyward. I see the wide sprawl of the Red River that threads its way down out of China and across Vietnam to the sea, and I think of where I've come from and where I'm going.

23

The air is a shock. Cold like I haven't felt for a long time, biting and blowing at my skin. The night sky is dark wool, cut with a glow from the ground. I stand on the steps of the plane and I can taste England in the air: the sharp salt sweetness of what I remember – what I was – mixed with what I am.

The journey was shit. Sour sweat, burnt coffee, sleeping curled on plastic seats with my knees up to my chin. And hassle – real hassle – in India when no one seemed to know who we were and what we were doing: thirty-six hours in an airless holding room in the airport until a British official could be bothered to come out and sign us off. And always the problem was me. I had no passport, no record of where I'd come from or what I was about. I was strip-searched in Istanbul in spite of Yeo's protestations, by a man-mountain called Enver who had hairs on the palms of his hands. My blood's been taken and tested in India, and then again in Turkey. They wouldn't let me off the plane until the results were clear.

We're in a small airfield near Cobham in Surrey – I know because I heard the pilot talking – a trimmed lawn slopes away from us, silver in the darkness. In the distance, I see house lights like stars under suburban slate and brick. It chokes and jolts me all over again.

Then headlight beams light up strips on the grass. A black Range Rover swings up in front of us and a man gets out. The cold air carries his scent across to me: smoke and leather. He's tall and dressed in army uniform and he rubs his hands together and folds his arms against the cold. Yeo peels around me and taps down the steps towards him. I back up, sit down on the top step and watch them talk. I can't follow it – I don't want to – I could care less what they're talking about. Nothing seems real anymore. All I can see when I close my eyes is the fighting cage and bodies I've broken in it or around it. And I'm thinking how I can ever really be here – be normal – get a job or a TV licence or whatever, when there's all this knocking about in my head?

'Time to go,' calls Yeo, and I get up and clang down the steps to where they're waiting. Yeo stands by the car and the man steps forward to greet me. 'Hello, I'm Colonel Keeling. So you're Ben? Mr Yeo has briefed me. Can't quite believe it, I must say.'

I look at him. He's about fifty I reckon, with a ramrod back and a long neck. He looks at me fascinated, like he's waiting for me to tip my eyeballs out and start juggling with them. I say, 'Yeah. Yeah. It's all true.'

'Your father was –'

'Yeah. He's the guy.'

He fixes me with searching eyes. 'What was he like? Your father? I heard of him at Porton Down years ago.'

I think of the picture. The dark woods. 'He was … lost … I don't know.' He nods but he doesn't get it. I don't even know if I do.

'Yes,' he says quietly. 'Yes, but was he –?'

I see him catch a look from Yeo and he turns back and climbs into the front seat and sits in silence as we pull away. I look back at the plane that brought me here, like a white worm in the dark field.

24

Sophy

The letter said they were watching me, that I was next. I tore it into tiny pieces and phoned Josh late last night but he didn't answer. There's nothing like the darkness when you're alone in a house. It's fat and thick, enveloping. I couldn't risk a candle after that, so I did the best I could to barricade the doors and windows and I spent the night on the landing with the loaded gun while the house whispered and roosted around me. I'm seeing things. I saw Lily, I know I did: her heel rounding a corner, a dimpled hand on a door handle, the brush of her baby hair against my face.

And I sat there and bawled my eyes out.

I'm starting to feel like the last person on the planet. I know why. No one's going to come anywhere near me now they know about Lily. And the white sheet is still hanging and flapping outside the house.

I know why Josh won't answer my calls. It's about Ben. Of course. It all got a bit crazy after Ben called.

Maurice sloped off and left us to it. Josh was upset – not upset – just angry with me, with Ben, about everything and I tried but we both knew. He'd seen me on the phone, afterwards. He said, 'I don't stand a chance. You made me think …' and all that, which I said wasn't true but thinking about it now, maybe I did, maybe I did lead him on.

I didn't mean to, except maybe I did … maybe I wanted to feel something that wasn't totally hopeless and stuck, and he did that for me. And if Ben hadn't … if it weren't for how I feel about Ben, still, then maybe we would have had a chance. I like Josh and I said so, but telling someone you 'like' them: that's always the last thing they're going to want to hear when they feel something more.

It got nasty, then uncomfortable, then quiet, and after a while, after we'd sat at the kitchen table and I'd reached out what I thought was a friendly hand, he'd snatched his away and pushed his chair back and slammed out of the house.

That was two days ago. The last time I spoke to anyone. And then this letter arrived yesterday. I heard it flop onto the mat and footsteps falling away on the tarmac. The Reapers know about me.

And I'm sure now where I wasn't before, that Mum and Dad are dead. The Reapers don't pull their punches. My neighbour told me yesterday they'd heard of a body found by the canal, a young man, badly burned and wrapped in polythene. And on his back, scored into the skin, the words, 'PUNISHED'.

I have to get out.

I sit in the dark with a piece of paper and I write. Something. Anything. To him:

> *Ben*
> *If you ever see this, if you read this, don't bother looking for me. I'll probably be dead. I just want you to know I've thought about you every day since I last saw you. And hearing your voice again was wonderful.*
> *I hope you get home.*
> *I love you.*
> *Sophy.*
> *P.S. look after Maurice.*

The sound of the pen on the paper, the words that it's too dark to see, the crease as I fold it, all reach and comfort me.

I'm going to get across town to Maurice. I know the house is being watched, so I'm going to have to go in the dark, late.

The day drags and slides. Heavy grey clouds and a fine mist in the air. I keep the gun by my side all the time, and where at first it freaked me out, now it comforts me, the weight of it, the fat bullets cradled in its dark cavities. I wasn't lying to Maurice – I know

I can use this. I wouldn't hesitate. Right now I'm so wired I can feel every muscle pulling and twitching under my skin. My head aches and my mouth is so dry it hurts to swallow. All I can think about is surviving. One more hour, one more day.

I wonder where he is now. What he meant by 'I can cure this …' I wonder who's with him, whether they're good people.

I don't think I'm scared of dying anymore. Not after Lily. Not after all this.

I just wanted to see him again, hear his voice.

It's dark outside. I get ready to go.

25

Dawn's breaking.

The car stalls on the filter lane towards the motorway. Once, twice. Keeling turns to me. 'Petrol shortage. We're using rape oil. It's not perfect but it does the job, most of the time.'

Yeo shoots a look at me, raises an eyebrow.

After a minute or two, the engine turns over, and we pull away onto the M3. Apart from a tank division coming up the other way, it's empty – miles and miles of dark tarmac stretching ahead of us. The central reservation barriers are crushed and twisted and missing in places. I go to open a window but Keeling stops me and shakes his head. We drive on as daylight takes hold. I'm looking ahead when Keeling shouts at the driver: 'Look out, man!'

A dark shape – two dark shapes – in the road. The car swerves and I turn to see. A man and a boy standing in the road, both stripped to the waist, their faces turned upwards and their arms waving and clawing wildly at the sky.

'What the –?' I say.

Yeo and I look at him. He says, 'They're infected. Late stage. They live on the motorways. That's what the tank patrols are for.'

'*They*?'

'They,' he echoes, and then, pointing, says, 'look. Slow down, Tim.' The driver slows as we come to a bridge across the road. The first thing I see is light from a brazier and then shadows cast up high on the concrete. Nine or ten figures, some standing and gesticulating like the two we saw before, some curled and twitching on the ground and above on the bridge, silhouetted against the sky, people naked to the waist staring upwards, their bodies covered in dark boils.

'Looks like they're waiting for something,' I say.

I hear Yeo swallow. 'Yes,' he says, 'this is the end stage, the spores are about to explode.'

Keeling leans to the driver. 'Alright. Enough. Let's go.' The sound of sirens fills the air and the car speeds away. I hold my head in my hand and try to think about the future, any future.

We're driving another hour, swerving or slowing as the sick figures lurch on and off the road. After a while we turn off the motorway and I sit up straight in my seat. The sign is there but scratched and faded, the little stag crest and the name above it: Rees.

26

'Yes,' says Keeling as we pull up. A trio of heavily armed soldiers in full Biohazard gear greet us and wave us through. 'I ... Rees is pretty much the only place left in the South East that has the technology, the labs, the manufacturing side too.'

The outside walls are pitted with holes and some of the glass is cracked or broken. Those revolving doors are still there but the reception is staffed by soldiers in full body armour and masks. All are armed.

'This way,' says Keeling, and we follow him past piles of empty boxes, office chairs and mangled in-trays, through a door to the stairs. 'Lifts are a little shaky.'

We travel down stairway after stairway. Nobody talks. The only sound comes from the clatter of our feet on the metal treads.

At the bottom of the stairs we reach a reinforced door and Keeling pushes a finger against a pad in the wall and the door grinds open onto a long white corridor. There's no one about, and apart from a hum from the strip lights above us, there's no sound either. There's a kind of heaviness in the air which I guess comes from being so far underground. Way away at the end of the corridor is a sort of grille over a steel door that's riveted into the wall.

'What's in there?' I ask as we move along the corridor.

'You don't want to know,' says Keeling. And before I have time to ask any more, he turns off and goes through a door into a small glass washroom that looks out onto an operating theatre. A man comes forward to greet us. He's thin with longish grey hair tucked behind his ears. His eyes glitter behind thick glasses. He pushes out his hand. 'Ben, is it? I'm Dr Conway. Let's get started.'

Strip lights here too. Harsh and sharp. I lie down on the trolley, close my eyes and listen. I feel the pinch of a needle in my hand and a line is pushed into a vein. Almost at once, vivid shapes loom and dance behind my eyes. I let myself drift but still I can hear them, the buzz of voices close by: Keeling's there, talking in his clipped military snap: 'He did it. Incredible. Got to admire the chap. In a way. What he did. Incredible. It's so single bloody minded. And the boy ...'

'Mmm,' I hear Conway, the rustle of his scrubs above me. 'He certainly covered all the bases.'

There's silence and then Keeling says, 'This thing ... I know this isn't an ordinary virus ... I mean, it's ...' he tails off and he's waiting.

Conway mutters something, or maybe he's just clearing his throat, then he says, 'Of course, there's no such thing as an *ordinary* virus but no, you're right. No. It's a ... a kind of hybrid. We know now the virus has been modified to contain some fungal DNA: fungal genes.'

'And you know how –'

'Well, thanks to Mr Yeo, yes. We know now. The fungus is a bastardised version of something called the Cordyceps, or 'club head' fungus: nasty beast. It's a parasite. Attacks insects. It invades the host, destroys it from the inside out and grows inside it. It affects the behaviour of the host before it kills it – completely alters its mind – sends it mad. The one he's based this on attacks ants. It makes them want to climb up high before they die.'

Keeling gives a low whistle. 'Christ! That's why –'

'Yes ... that's why they do it: in the later stages, people have this impulse, this urge, to climb. They can't help it – it's the fungus.'

'But why would it ...?'

'Obvious: maximum distribution of spores. Once the host is dead, the fungus breaks through the skin. It fruits. Unimaginable ability to infect others over a huge area.'

'Good Lord.'

'The virus itself is just the carrier, you see, it's what gets into the cells and effectively hijacks them, manipulates them, and allows the fungus to take over. That's what's so clever about it.'

He walks away and I turn my head slowly in the direction of the sound. I hear liquid being poured against glass and strain to hear as he continues. 'I know he stopped work on it but whoever weaponised it would have probably aerosolised it so people would just breathe it in and pass it on. It would go straight into the lining of the lungs, blood vessels, liver. Wholesale impact.'

'God.'

Conway's back standing over me. My eyes and mouth are dry and my tongue is furred.

I feel like I'm desiccating. Drifting. He's talking to me: 'We're going to take some bone marrow. Can you hear me, Ben?' Dr Conway brushes a gloved hand against my face.

I nod, at least I feel like I'm nodding. The space in my head is blue and cold. Blue and cold. Like toothpaste. Another voice – urgent, breathless: it's Yeo: 'You saw it? The code?'

'I did. Extraordinary. What a thing to do,' says Conway. And he lowers his voice to a whisper. 'Does he know?'

Nothing. No sound but the clink and clatter of instruments.

When I wake up I'm lying on my front, naked to the waist, my bad arm tucked under me. There's a dull pain deep in my bones. Keeling's talking: 'Fascinating. Absolutely fascinating,' he's saying. I feel hot breath on my skin. I twist around to see Conway above me.

'What are you doing?' I say.

'One minute. Just give us a minute. Nearly finished,' Dr Conway says, and his grey eyes light on me for a second and look away.

Yeo comes around to face me. 'You OK, Ben? Bit sore?' I nod. 'It's where we took your bone marrow. It'll be sore like a bruise for few days.' He nods encouragingly.

'Will it be OK?' I ask, craning my neck. 'I mean, what you've got, what you've taken? How long till you can make the —?'

I see Yeo look at Dr Conway behind me, his eyes wide, his mouth open. 'You can turn over now,' he says.

'Clever. Very clever,' says Dr Conway nodding at Yeo. I turn and hunch up on the table. 'What? What's clever?'

Conway pulls off his gloves and says to Yeo, 'Will you tell him or will I?'

Yeo looks away and mutters, 'You tell.'

That blackness again: I'm back in the cage. It takes me by surprise. I raise myself onto my elbow. 'What is it?'

He puts a hand on my arm, firm and cold, but not unkind, and I lie back. 'The tattoo,' says Conway.

'What about it?' I say. I see his flint eyes flick from Keeling to Yeo and back to me. He folds his arms. 'The snake tattoo. It wasn't just decorative you know. In the scales, in the coils he's hidden the code to make the —'

I stare at him. 'Code?'

'OK. Um …' He paces away and back, never taking his eyes off me. 'You have antibodies in your blood to this thing right? Your cells have what we call a "memory". That's what makes you immune to this thing. They ... remember it, they recognise it, so they can defend against it. Over the years he was ... injecting you, he made it.'

'Jesus.'

He goes on: 'So ... you're immune. So when we harvest your bone marrow we get cells carrying the antibody. But, the antibodies in themselves aren't enough. We need to understand what it is in this virus-fungus that your antibodies will recognise and attack. Every gene, and there are hundreds of thousands of them, has its own unique ... er ... make-up – its "code", if you like, and these are represented by a series of letters, all different combinations, and it's that that gives us the blueprint for the protein we want to isolate in the fungus, the one that's doing the damage. Once we've done that, then we can test it with your antibodies to make a vaccine.'

I can hear the words but the blackness is still hanging about me like a fog. I ball and clench my fists and the urge to feel them on bone and flesh, any bone, any flesh, is huge. He adds, 'And that's what's in the tattoo: the code sequence for the right protein.'

'And then what?' I say.

'Rees ... er ... they were close, very close. Now we have the code, your DNA, we can make this thing on a large scale.'

'How are you going to deliver it? Get it out there?'

A look passes between Keeling and Conway.

'There's a way,' says Conway. 'In fact it's actually down to Rees. They didn't quite have the vaccine right but they'd certainly nailed a means of dispersal.'

'How?'

'Oh, it's clever, very clever. If we have time I can show you …'

'No. You're OK. As long as it works,' I say.

'Yes. It'll work. I'm sure of that,' says Conway. 'We simply wrap the vaccine in a capsular coat, protect it till it gets to where it needs to be and let it go.'

Keeling's standing with his back against the wall but he looks up then and says, 'Did you hear that?' We all turn and follow his gaze. There's a tinny whine coming from way above us.

'It's probably nothing,' says Conway, and he turns to me. 'Ben. I can't imagine how you must feel, what you've been through, but –'

I look past him. There's only one person who can save me. 'Can someone get me my clothes?'

27

Sophy

The streets are deserted. My feet scrape on wet ground and now and again, the dark paths brighten as a street light fizzes into life. I follow my breath in the darkness, feeling the gun against my side.

Every so often, I stop. I pull in against brick and flatten myself, trying to slow my breathing, to swallow and wet my mouth. I wait and I listen. For footsteps, an echo, a fox barking, a dry cough. But there's nothing, only the silent rain, soft on my face and my own footsteps moving over pavement. Step by step. Stay in the lines. I used to play that when I was little. Stay in the lines and the bears won't get you. Stay in the lines, and you'll be safe.

I reach the London Road and cut across the car forecourt as before. Tin cans and bottles clatter and roll in front of me and hawthorn spines tear at my clothes as I push through into the alleyway. I stop again when I'm through and listen. Nothing. Then a faint scratching, a pushing, away to my left on the ground. Rats.

There's no light in the alley. I pick my way through towards his place. A sharp sound then, a creaking whine stops me in my tracks. I hold my breath. Regular now: the sound is coming from Maurice's. I bring the gun up, tight against my shoulder, and move towards the noise. A faint lick of candlelight through his window shows me what I can hear: his front door is hanging open off its hinges and swinging drunkenly back and forth against the frame. I freeze.

I wait. I hold my breath and I wait. The gun in my hand is hot and heavy and I shift under it. But my finger stays hooked and steady on the trigger. The candle blinks and flickers like an eye in the dark, and the door wheezes on its hinges. And then I hear a faint noise, something behind the sound of the door. A dragging sound, a soft pull. And then it stops, and I'm not sure I heard it at all.

I look back down the alley at the torn weeds and broken stones snaking into darkness. And all the time, I'm straining to hear, to see something. I look back at Maurice's open doorway and back again. Suddenly there's a crash, and a moment later, a thin shadow crosses my field of vision, then another, both jump the steps from his place and run. I raise the gun and aim but they're too quick: dark hoodies, thick trainers, running fast away up the alley.

I hear a muted crackling sound from behind me and I turn back to Maurice's. There are flames licking up the curtains, catching at cloth and paper. Quickly, the doorway fills with heat and light, illuminating the broken brickwork and rubbish. The paint on the walls has run but it's fresh and clear: 'PUNISHED' daubed in giant capitals. A rat runs for cover over my feet. I go to run too but then I hear a cry from inside.

'Help me!'

I make myself, I force myself to walk towards the flames. My body's rigid. I can't feel my arms or legs. There's heat around my heart, my chest, but everywhere else is numb and cold. I cradle the gun across my body and walk.

Red heat and black behind it. It coughs its way into my head, pumps itself into my nose and mouth. Panic overcomes me and I start to back away but the cry comes again: 'Please?'

It's Maurice. I scan the room. Head height, waist height, there's nothing.

'Help!'

Fainter now, but it's coming from the floor. I leave the gun and get to my knees and crawl. His sofa's on fire, belching grey clouds of smoke. I scream, 'Maurice! Where are you?'

A hand meets my hand, soft and fleshy and strangely cold. He's lying behind the sofa, a vast dark mass. He coughs out my name, 'Sophy?'

'Maurice! Are you OK? Can you stand? We have to get out.'

'Help me,' is all he says. And his meaty fingers curl over mine. I get to my feet and try to pull him but he's too heavy. He lifts his head and it sinks back to the floor with a thud. Thick smoke is swirling about our heads and there's the snapping and cracking of broken glass from behind him. I say again, 'Come on! Maurice please! You have to help me! I can't do this! Please!'

He groans and splutters, 'Can't.'

'What happened?'

'Reapers. Bastards. My legs.'

'Your legs?'

He's breathless now, talking in short gasps, 'Battered me. Cut me. Broke my legs with a tyre iron.'

My eyes are streaming and it hurts to breathe. I kick at the sofa to shift it and the arm falls off sending burning dust into the room. I make some space, then take Maurice's hands in mine, and with all my strength, I pull at him. I move him about an inch before we both collapse. From us to the door is about fifteen feet. Flames are crawling over the door frame into the small kitchen. I get my breath, then bend again to pull him,

'Maurice, come on, you have to help me!' I'm shouting at him. He struggles again to raise his head and starts to pull himself on his elbows. I get on the floor to help him and pushing and pulling between us, we move another foot or two. I can feel the smoke inside me, in my blood. I know I can't stay in here much longer and survive but I know if I leave him he'll be dead.

I pull off my jacket and cover his head to stop the smoke getting to him and grab his wrists and pull. And I don't stop pulling. Suddenly it's easier – Maurice is moving fast over the floor. There's the nudge of someone at my side – arms and shoulders hauling with me, until we're out, away from the crowded, choking dark of the room into the night, and I'm on the step, gulping air like a fish. Maurice is on the ground next to me, and the figure kneeling over him, who looks back at me with wide eyes, is Ben.

28

I never felt so bad. Never. Not even after the fight with Tiger when I had to crawl through that tunnel with a broken arm. My head's buzzing. All the time. A low, thick drumming between my ears that pushes its way into my throat and my chest. And under my skin, on muscle and bone, there's pain. Conway said it would go after a few days. Like I have a few days. Like I'm going to go to bed with an aspirin and read a fucking book.

He watches me as I get dressed. 'What will you do?'

I reset my sling, look up at him. 'Why?'

'I just … I wondered …'

'I'm going to see the people who thought I was dead,' I say. 'I'm going to tell them that you're making a vaccine. What else?'

He opens his mouth to speak and then closes it tight with a snapping sound. Then he says quietly, 'I see.'

'You are, aren't you?'

'Making a vaccine? Yes. It looks good – the code, your antibodies – a perfect match. We should have the first batch in a matter of days.'

'Then what are you waiting for?' I say, 'I'm going.'

He stops me at the door. 'Ben.'

'What?'

'I'd be very careful about who you tell.'

I look at him. But he doesn't meet my eyes. He goes on: 'The vaccine, we don't want to create panic about news like that … with desperate people, you understand me?'

I nod. 'I get it.'

'Thank you,' he says, 'I … you've been very brave … and very …' he falters here and I think I maybe see tears in his eyes. 'I hope one day you'll be able to put this behind you and find – I don't know – happiness. Good luck.' He puts out his hand and I take it. His palm is firm and dry.

I say, 'Thanks. Thank you.'

He hands me a phone. 'Take this. They don't always work but keep trying, and call me if you need anything. My number's in it.'

He steps back to let me pass and later on when I'm outside, I look back up at where I've come from and I see him, his head bent over a bench in his lab, his glasses on the end of his nose.

They give me a hundred pounds. It's enough. They get me a car all the way home. I sit in the back seat and watch as we pass army trucks, road blocks, burning cars at the side of the road, empty streets and shops, and houses with what look like white flags or sheets hanging from the eaves.

It's getting dark when the driver drops me at the top of my road. And the first house I come to has a white bed sheet looped about the guttering and flapping against the brick. All of the windows are barred with planks of wood and in the front garden, the earth is rutted and potholed like a giant mole's been at it. They used to have gnomes and a pond.

All that's growing there is the apple tree: fat, with a twisted trunk and crisping leaves. I almost miss it but something makes me look up. In amongst the reds and browns, just visible between the crusted boughs, hangs a body. And making its way up the tree trunk in dark lettering burned into the bark, the word: Punished.

I start to run. I get into the road and I start running like I've never run before, round the bend and up the hill and along the flat. I pass houses I grew up with, all changed, all dark, boarded up, until I get to my house.

Someone's written a sign outside saying, KEEP OUT. The garden at the front is in furrows, like a ploughed field, and all around it, there are coils of barbed wire. An army jeep is parked at an angle across the drive. I stand in front of the place for a moment, slowing my breathing and listening to my heart in my chest. I can see the window to his study. I can see the garage where I found him. I can see the upstairs window from where I crouched and watched the street that night. I want more than anything to leave him outside, back in China, blood and dust on that forest floor.

A cry from across the street brings me to my senses. It's a woman. Her voice is harsh and sharp: 'Oi! There's a loaded gun pointed right at you! Right now! You've got sixty seconds to turn around and start walking. Get out!'

I turn towards the sound and instinctively raise my hands.

'Ben?'

A voice, a whisper close behind me makes me jump. 'Karen?'

'It's OK Mrs Pryce,' she's shouting, 'it's my nephew.'

'Karen?' All I feel is hot tears on my face.

A step and the touch of her on my shoulder, my back, my neck. I'm choking.

'Ben,' she says, gently.

I turn around then and I'm holding her. She's small – bird bones. She smells of home and of something that's maybe still there for me. There's nothing to say now, I don't need words. The smell and the sound of home is enough. And then: 'I don't believe it!' Charlie's feet behind Karen. 'Sophy called – we didn't know when to expect you – Karen's been camped out here all night.'

Heavy boots. And his hand, the weight of it.

I face him. 'You're OK? You're both OK?'

He nods. 'You? What have you done to your arm?'

I step up close to him. 'I'll tell you later. But Dad … he was there. Still alive. He was … he was making an vaccine for this. All along … he needed me to –'

'What?' he says. '*What*? Am I hearing you right? Dad's alive? So where is he now?'

I shake my head. 'He was going to come with me but he –' and then I start to think maybe he wasn't. He was never going to come home – how could he? He was always going to do what he did one way or the other. I say, 'He died back in China.'

His mouth hangs open, then he pulls me into him. 'Jesus, Ben. What you've been through … you're an idiot. I told you not to go.'

'No,' I say. 'No, I'm glad. I saw him, spent time with him. And fuck it, because I went, there's a vaccine for this thing.'

'I thought you said he destroyed it?'

'No,' I smile. 'That's where I came in. The … vaccine, the antibodies to this virus, they're in my blood, they've been there all along. He … put them there years ago and … That's why he needed me. To … finish it. He got me out of China just in time.'

He walks away, then back. 'You're fucking with my head. You are seriously fucking with me …'

'I know, mate. I couldn't tell you before … but I knew. He left a letter. I couldn't tell anyone what he'd done. Couldn't deal. But I think they're close to finding something – a cure. They started working on me when I got back.'

'*Working on you*? Where?'

I look at him. 'Rees.'

'Rees? What, *the* Rees?'

I nod. 'Well, it's not like it was. But they've got the labs to make it in and disperse it.'

He nods slowly but his mouth's still wide open. Karen's staring too. She looks twenty years older. I ask her, 'That house at the end of the road ... there's a body...'

'I know,' she says. 'Mr Austin. His wife got this thing: the disease. They find you ... if you've been in contact with it − they're trying to root it out.'

'*They*? Who's they?'

Charlie says, 'A kind of vigilante group called the Reapers. People are shit scared. They're all over the place, groups like this ... anyone shows any sign of illness and the whole family's in trouble.'

I listen, watching him, hearing him, remembering him and then what he's saying actually sinks in. 'Sophy.'

'Too late, mate.'

'What? I thought ... I only −'

'No. No. I mean it's too late to go out now.'

'What? Why?'

'Er ... have you looked around you? Do things *look* normal? There's a curfew. No one out after dark. End of.'

'Fuck that,' I say.

'Ben ... don't,' he calls but he sees my face. Then he says, 'I'll give you a lift.'

'No, you're OK. Stay with Karen.'

I give them both a hug and I turn and run back down the road. I run to Sophy's house. My throat jams when I see the white sheet against the house.

It's dark inside and I can see things have been wedged against the doors to keep people out. I jump the garden door at the side and go around the back. Like at my house, every bit of grass is gone and there are ploughed ditches and furrows in the earth. I try the doors, and when I get no luck, I break a window. There are boards against it but they've been fixed with thin nails. It's the work of seconds to push them out of the way and climb in over the sill into the silent house. I creep up the stairs to her room. There are clothes and boxes on the floor making odd hunched shapes in the moonlight.

I sit on her bed, and in the dark, in the quiet, I say her name softly. Just to hear it. The moon fills the room with its eerie whiteness. On the floor by my feet, I see a square of paper with my name across it.

Ben

If you ever see this, if you read this, don't bother looking for me. I'll probably be dead. I just want you to know I've thought about you every day since I saw you. And hearing your voice again was wonderful.

I hope you get home.

I love you.

Sophy.

P.S. look after Maurice.

I pull it into my fist and I breathe hard. I don't think. I pace the rest of the house, room to room, cupboard to cupboard. Then downstairs to the kitchen where I find two shotgun bullets on the table.

I leave the dark house, her note still in my hand, and I pick up and run. Across town to Maurice's place. I figure if she's alive, then maybe that's where she'll be – I hope.

I'm close when I smell burning. Two guys push past me as I round into the alley. And there, at the end, is Maurice's flat, where flames and black smoke are pushing out of the open door. I run. Every door and every window everywhere in the town is closed. There'll be no one to help.

I pull off my jumper, bind it across my face and walk into the smoke.

29

Sophy

His face in the half light is white and drawn. He hardly seems to see me. I feel weirdly shy. Maurice is dipping in and out of consciousness, gasping for air, his mouth and nose are black with ash and his chest is covered in blood. We turn him on his side and he begins to cough. I watch him and somehow I can't see Ben anymore. All I can see, all I can feel, is anger and hate and a deep, welling sadness for the whole lot of us. I stand up and turn away up the alley where broken bricks like tombstones force up through shining puddles.

'Sophy.'

I turn and he's there, and I'm in his arms. He folds me into him and he traces my skin with blackened hands, and with the lightest touch he runs a finger across my lips.

'Your arm …' I say.

'It's OK.'

'Ben. I never thought –'

'Don't talk,' he says and his hands are in my hair. He leans to kiss me, lightly at first, then with a force that takes my breath away. It's like he's pushing himself back into me, finding me again. I hold on to him, listening to his breathing, and mine, and all the numbness, the coldness I've felt for so long starts to leave me: I uncurl, I stretch myself against him. That rawness, that prickling, shivering heat I used to feel with him is coming back. I'm waking up.

'Bugger.' It's Maurice. We go to him. 'Bugger, bugger, bugger, bugger …' he's saying. Ben drops to the floor. I can still feel his fingers on me.

'Maurice. It's me, Ben.'

Maurice rolls himself up a little and wipes a hand across his mouth. He looks from me to Ben and back again. 'Bloody Hell. It is you, you bugger. Back from the dead.'

Ben takes out a phone and makes a call, and while he does, I see Maurice watching me. There's so much blood and his legs are buckled and twisted in front of him but he winks at me. 'Happy?'

I look at Ben. 'Yes,' I whisper.

Ben comes back. 'I just called my brother. He's going to come for us. I'll ask him to take you to hospital.'

Maurice and I stare at him, and Maurice says, 'I don't think so, mate.'

'The hospitals are just …' I say. 'They're just quarantine stations really. It'd be crazy to go to one if you're not sick.'

He looks at us. 'Well, where *do* you go?'

'He can come to mine,' I say. 'I'll … I'll look after him.'

'S'alright,' says Maurice, and he starts to squirm and wriggle like he's going to get up, 'You don't want me there if … when your folks get back.'

Ben's eyes are wide. 'Yeah, where *are* your Mum and Dad? They haven't –?'

I don't want to explain because it's all I can do all the time not to think about it.

Maurice is shaking his head. 'They'll be back. When all this blows over,' he says.

Ben ignores him and comes to me and takes my face in his hands. 'Where are they, Soph?'

'They were … this group took them when we were in hospital, when Lily was sick.'

'The Reapers?'

'Yeah. How did you …?'

He shakes his head and fixes me with his dark eyes. 'We'll find them. We will. Because all this is going to end. I promise.'

A battered army jeep crashes into the alley. Ben's brother, Charlie's driving. His face is white at the wheel. He comes straight over and hugs me. 'Jesus. Sophy,' is all he'll say.

At my place, they carry Maurice in and put him on the sofa. He keeps zoning out then pulling himself back.

I boil some water while they cut his clothes off him. On his chest, are jagged cuts in the flesh, and I can make out the beginnings of the word, "Punished".

Charlie has painkillers and a few bandages, and we tear up sheets for the rest. Only one of his legs is broken, and we make a splint from a table leg and a crutch from a broom handle. I make pasta and Maurice laps it up, oil running from his chin.

'I need to go to see to the house,' says Charlie. 'I'll be back in the morning – see if I can get hold of something to set that leg. You two going to be OK here?'

Ben and I look at each other and at Maurice who's drifting into sleep, chest and jowls heaving and trembling. 'Yeah,' we say together. And I think I catch a wink from Charlie that's meant for Ben. 'Course you will,' he says.

It's cold in here. Outside there's a thin moon and wet on the wind. I can feel it, feel winter pushing at us in this poor, blighted, messed up world, and all of us in it scared to death. But I'm here now with the man I looked for and wanted and dreamed about. And he's holding me, and he's taking my hand and leading me upstairs. It feels like a hundred years since we were last here together, so much has happened, we've got so much to tell each other and so much to learn but all I want now is him. His body on me and in me.

'You've changed,' he's saying.

'I'm thinner, older,' I say. 'I'm just tired, I guess.'

'I don't mean that – that doesn't mean anything. It's … in you.'

'Lily … losing her was –'

He closes his eyes, sits on the bed. 'I don't know what to say. Sorry isn't even close. I just –'

'It wasn't your fault.'

'Yeah, but this thing – you know this was … this started with my dad. This … he did this. He made it. I'm a part of that.'

'You're a part of him – that's not the same thing.'

'Maybe. But … because of him – I can do something about it. Something good.'

'What d'you mean?'

He gets up, comes close. 'Can I tell you later? My head's been so full of it for so long and now I just want to …   Fuck it, I don't know. Can I? Is this OK?'

He's teasing my straps down my arms, brushing my shoulders with his long fingers, one hand half out of his plaster cast. I'm shivering and I'm smiling and my mouth is wet and dry at the same time. He pulls off his T-shirt and his chest swells. The muscle under his skin is tight, turned, like wood and covered in welts and scars. I reach up and pull him to me and mouth to mouth, I breathe myself into him. He pulls off my shirt and his hands are on me, pressing and caressing; he half lifts me, half pushes me onto the bed, and he's on top of me. 'Sophy,' he's saying, 'Sophy …'

I look up and I can see the moon.

Much, much later I'm woken by the sound of a phone ringing and Ben reaching onto the floor for it. He answers it, listens, turns to me and strokes my face but he's far away again.

He's up then and pulling on his clothes. 'I've got to go.'

30

I cannot catch a break. Just when I want to wake up with Sophy, just when I want to wake up and make love to her again, the outside world just can't leave me alone. Leaving her once sucked, but this is the worst.

'Why?' she says, and her hair is all over the pillow and I can smell it on myself. I watch her, the crook of her elbow, and the round of her breasts under the sheet.

'It's ... it's to do with this vaccine, I have to go back to Rees. Something's happened, they wouldn't say – got cut off – but they need me. Will you be OK?'

Instead of answering and staying put, she gets up and starts getting dressed, and there's something about the way she's doing it that tells me she's not happy.

'I'm sorry,' I say.

'What for?' she snaps, and she's not looking at me, she's pulling her boots on.

'Well,' I say, 'I'm sorry I have to go ... if I –'

She stops and stares at me.

'Sophy, why are you getting up? It's not … it's still dark. You don't –'

'If you think – even for a moment – that you're going off without me, after all that's happened, after all I went through, you must be mad. Or stupid. I'm coming with you.'

I shake my head but I know I'm beaten. 'But you don't, it's not … I …'

She folds her arms. 'How were you going to get there?'

'I was going to call Charlie,' I say.

'There's another thing you didn't know about me.'

'What?'

'Come on.' I follow her downstairs and through the living room where Maurice is sleeping, and into the kitchen. She grabs a scarf and wraps it around her face. Carefully she lifts the latch.

I send a text to Charlie to look in on Maurice. I send it again and again and it's finally delivered.

The cold air hits me as I cross the driveway after her to an old Volvo Estate car parked on the kerb.

'Next-door neighbour's,' she whispers. 'I've watched him bury his keys.' She drops to her knees in the half-dark, and pushes at the turned soil, and after a bit of digging, she pulls up a smooth black stone with a key ring bored into it and a key.

'You can drive?'

'Come on,' she hisses, 'people are light sleepers.'

Sure enough, as the engine thrums into life, a light goes on in a house across the road. Sophy floors the pedal and swings the car around.

Soon we're pulling up onto the motorway.

And all the way, as we drive, strung out along the central reservation, there are people walking, heads down against the cold. All are wearing masks of some sort, some medical, some wraps and scarves. They're holding sticks and planks of wood; and in the headlights I see the glint of a gun barrel in someone's hand and the flash of a knife.

'I thought there was supposed to be a curfew?' I say.

'There is. I don't understand,' she says, and she reaches across for me and I feel her hand against mine, her fingers locking into my fingers.

We go on in silence till we pull off the motorway, and at the top of the filter lane by the roundabout, we see more people, hundreds, some carrying staves and poles that beat an ugly tattoo against the tarmac. Behind us, the army of people from the motorway are threading their way up towards them. She pulls up her scarf, wraps it tighter around her face, and winds down the window. 'What's going on?' she calls to anyone listening.

'Rees – Bastards – it's just now all over the Internet – they've got the vaccine, they've made a cure,' says a thin man under a tartan scarf. 'And we're going to get it before those fuckers can sell it.'

She winds the window back up and pulls down her scarf. Her face is white. 'Jesus, Ben. Is this what we're here for? They ... Rees are going to –'

'No! No, you don't understand, there is no Rees. There are people in there who want to fix this, who've been working to make a cure. But like I said, they needed me. I was the … the missing link. They needed my blood, my antibodies, and they need me again. I don't know about all this, these people – someone must have said something – put something online. The thing is, these guys are so close to finishing it, but if they're attacked, if the building's totalled, there won't be any cure at all.'

But Sophy's not listening. 'Oh my God!' she breathes. 'Oh, my God! I don't believe it.'

She cranks up the handbrake and the car bounces to a stop. Before I can stop her she's out of the car and running into the crowd.

'Sophy! Wait!' I chase her into the throng of masked marchers and I lose her. I'm calling but it's dark and there's shouting and drumming and I'm fighting my way through them, elbows and fists. I feel my cast crack along my wrist again. People close in and I'm pushed forwards and I'm twisting my head but it's like a rip tide, I can't go back. There's a helicopter now, two helicopters overhead and they're sweeping us with lights. All I can see is heads and hands. And then, her voice in my ear: 'Ben.'

'Shit, Sophy, where did you go? You need to get back in the –'

But she's smiling, glowing, shining. And either side of her, are her Mum and Dad. Her Dad looks thin and wan and distant, and her Mum has dark lines around her eyes. She's holding tight onto Sophy. They're both wearing dirty masks and her Dad has a hunting knife in his belt.

'They were taken. They escaped. They thought I must be dead by now. They've been living rough for weeks, eating what they've scavenged, sleeping under hedges.'

Her mum nods. 'We got away from the Reapers soon after we were caught, we just kept running – got a lift with an army truck cross-country and ended up near Lincoln. Your father,' she says, looking at him, 'he's not the same – lost his mind after Lily's death, then you … he …'

'They came … they were frightened to go home … and then this – they heard about a vaccine.' There are tears in her eyes.

Lost and found. I watch her and I think about *my* Dad, his fists curled at his sides, the light in his eyes he had when he talked about what he loved. And all the happiness I felt with Sophy gets squeezed out of me for a second. Her mum's saying, 'Is it true then, about the cure? Sophy says you know something. They've got it?'

'Yes and no,' I say.

'What do you mean?'

I turn to Sophy. 'Sophy I'm happy for you, I really am, but I have to go.'

'I'm coming too.'

'No, you stay with your Mum and Dad.'

'We'll come with you,' says her Dad quietly. It's the first time he's spoken. Sophy looks from him to me, and I shake my head a fraction but it's her mum who says, 'No, Martin. They have to do this.'

'But I want to –'

'No,' she says again, laying a hand on his arm. The crowd is pressing forward and it carries us with it. Sophy's Mum says to me, 'Take her, you go. We'll be here Sophy. We love you.'

'I love you too,' she calls, and together we push forward into the night.

31

Rees is a mess. The fences are buckled and the wire is cut all along the perimeter. People mill about or just stand still stand looking up at it, their masks white like muzzles in the dark. A couple of soldiers watch them warily. Some lights flicker and gutter at high windows, in others I can see flames. The main crowd is still a way off but a little group of men run roaring past us towards the doors only to be pushed back. I pull Sophy back into shadow and call up Conway on the phone. It takes three attempts but finally he answers in a cracked whisper: 'Ben, where are you?'

'Just outside. You?'

'Here in the lower basement near where you left us. We're surrounded. The army knows. Everyone knows and it's too soon.'

'How? How did they find out?'

There's a silence and the phone line crackles. A breath. 'We thought we were so careful but … someone must have guessed, leaked it …'

'What do you need?'

'You. Come through the main way. Keeling will meet you. He's trying to keep his men in check but … Christ! What was that?' I hear it too, a sharp rattle of gun fire. 'Ben, hurry.' The line fizzes to a close and I take Sophy's hand.

'Just stay here. Please? I don't want you to get hurt, I …'

She looks at me. A grey dawn is just breaking and I see her face pale and resolute. She shakes her head once and starts for the door.

Inside it's worse than before. The marble floor is streaked with dirt; oil lamps steam on the old reception desk and piled high in every corner, along with discarded office furniture, black bags vomit heaps of shredded paper. A young soldier is leaning on the desk, his machine gun swings at his back.

'Excuse me?' I say.

He turns slowly and says, 'Sophy?'

'Josh!'

I stare at the two of them and a sick feeling catches me like cold hands on my throat.

'Ben,' she says. 'This is Josh.'

'Right,' I say.

'You remember him from school?' she tries. We look at each other, him and me.

'No,' I say, still looking at him.

'I remember you,' he says with a sneer. I'm back in that cage. Two minute's hand-to-hand and I could waste this guy. But I don't. I make an effort and turn to Sophy.

'Look, why don't you stay here with your friend? I won't be long.' And to him, I say, 'Let me through. I need to see Dr Conway.'

Josh gives me a look and I watch his knuckles shine and tighten on his gun. Just then Keeling appears. 'It's alright. He's with me, come this way.' He turns back to Sophy. 'Miss, you can't be in here. It's very dangerous. This young man will see you out.' He nods to Josh but Sophy says, 'No. No, I'm with Ben.' And she kind of says it to Josh as much as to Keeling and me.

Keeling looks at me. 'This true? *With* you? What does that mean?'

I say nothing but she says, 'I'm his … I'm with him and I'm not leaving without him.'

A commotion at the front draws Josh away for a moment. The crowds are getting close. Something's hurled at the glass doors and they shatter into thousands of pieces. Keeling grabs us both. 'Come on then. This way.'

We follow him down the way I went before. I can feel Sophy's hot breath on my neck as we run. There are soldiers stationed at every stairwell, and behind us and above us, the muffled sounds of stamping and banging.

Again, we open on to the long corridor where very little sound gets through. Two strip lights are out and others flicker and dim.

Keeling sounds odd. He's breathing heavily, and there's sweat on his neck. He strides to the end of the corridor, to the grille over the steel door, squares his shoulders and I see him flick his tongue across his upper lip.

He unlocks the grille and pulls it back. Sophy goes to hold my hand but I don't take it. Josh is still in my head and the more I think about it, the more I'm certain I recognise his voice from the phone.

He was with Sophy that night.

Keeling presses the key pad and the door begins to unlock itself. He turns to us. 'Not pretty, what you're going to see. Not … nice.'

I hear Sophy gasp quietly. I swallow. Nothing he could ever have said in a million years would have prepared me to see what was behind that door.

For a start, it's in semi-darkness. Not the kind of dark where the lights aren't working but the dark that's there for a reason. We step in, blinking to adjust to the gloom, and we're in a long, low chamber with an arched ceiling. At the end of the room, there's another door set slightly ajar, where a long arm of light spills across the floor.

There's a kind of hum that seems to come from everywhere and nowhere, a grinding engine noise that gets up in my head and stays there.

We stop and I find I'm holding my breath. The air in here is foul – clotted. There's none of the disinfectant tang of the other rooms I've seen down here.

Ranged along the walls on either side of a narrow aisle are a series of what look like tanks. They're set high on steel supports. There must be about thirty of them extending the length of the room.

'Just look ahead and keep walking,' says Keeling briskly.

But I can't do that.

Above us the ceiling is webbed with a network of pipes and cables that criss-cross and connect to the tanks below.

And the tanks.

Fuck.

The tanks are filled with a clear liquid, a viscous, gummy looking stuff that smells of pond weed, and suspended inside the liquid, are strange, bloated pinkish forms that twitch and roll and jerk. They're about four or five foot in length, a bit like seals, and all over them, like twisted limbs or branches, are tiny vestigial growths. On one, I see what looks like a hand with curled fingers and swollen knuckles; on another, a fleshy lump with a single row of white, human teeth. Another rolls and thrashes, and as it twists, I see an eye – one dark eye – pupils wide, flash a look at me and blink long wet lashes. The liquid around it sloshes against the sides of the tank and is still again.

The generator purrs above us and I can hear my feet on the floor.

Sophy whispers, 'What is this?'

Conway's voice comes out of the gloom towards us: 'I'm sorry you had to see this. It came out of ... a truly desperate attempt to create an effective vaccine.'

He doesn't meet my eye as he speaks. 'They're … er … Rees have been growing corrupted human cells in the tanks and trying to use them to create a blood serum as a base for the vaccine, just as your father did with you, Ben.'

'This is the sickest thing I've ever seen. Did Dad … did my father know?'

'No. No. They started this programme when he was working on his cancer treatment. This was the most covert operation. Most of the Rees staff didn't even know about this floor of the building.'

'Ben?' It's Sophy, urgent at my side.

I turn and her face is white. Keeling says then, 'Can we get out of here?'

'Yes, Yes, of course,' says Conway. 'And who's this?' he nods at Sophy, and I'm aware that Dr Yeo stands behind him, silhouetted by light from the open door. I look at Sophy. Her eyes are still fixed on Conway.

'I'm Sophy. I'm …' and she looks at me.

'She's my girlfriend,' I finish.

'Ah,' says Conway. 'Right. Well, come this way.'

'Ben!' she pulls me back, whispering: 'Do you trust them?'

I turn but Keeling's ushering me through the door, his hand against my back, and asking Conway, 'What's going to happen to these … these … things?'

'They'll be switched off in due course.'

'In due course? Why not now? It's grotesque.'

Conway leads us away and out of the chamber and into a well-lit lab before he answers. 'Not now because we still need them. Rees got very close using them. We haven't released this information, but in fact, they already had a sort of vaccine that might have a fairly good hit rate. But it wasn't good enough to sell you see. The people buying wanted absolute certainty before they went ahead.'

'I don't understand,' I say. 'You mean the terrorists? They've already gone ahead without a vaccine, haven't they?'

'My understanding is that unleashing this virus into the population was a unilateral act by a North Korean cell based in China. They acted, or they say they acted, without central government approval. All we can do now is to try to mitigate this, and quickly. That's why I called you back.'

He looks at Keeling who nods. I fold my arms and wait.

He says, 'OK. The vaccine's ready. We've worked all night on it. It's shaky, but it'll work. We took what we ... what Rees already had, and together with your antibodies and the coding from your father, we've made it. It'll be OK in water till people can ingest it. There's enough to go directly into the water system so enough people can get by till we can get a proper immunisation programme rolling. I've sent the codes to colleagues all over the world.'

'So what are you waiting for?'

His grey eyes flicker up at me then away. 'What we need now, is to release it.'

'And? Well, just do it then. What d'you need me for?'

'I can't do it.'

'Why?' I ask.

He pulls off his glasses and bends them in his fingers, rubs his eyes. 'I worked for Rees,' he says quietly. 'It's only a matter of time before someone recognises me. If I'm to make amends, make up for what … I have to be allowed to finish this.'

'What the fuck? So this is … you're –' I say.

He shakes his head. 'No. Not what you think. Not entirely. This project,' he waves his hand back at the tanks, 'all this, this … desperate work … I designed it. Rees threatened me like they threatened your father. I never knew him, I was recruited after he … after he left the project but I know – at least I can guess – what they did and said to him because they did exactly the same to me – my family.' He pauses and swallows hard. 'But I was a part of what made this thing – and in spite of what I've done since, people won't understand – I wouldn't expect them to. I can't be seen. We got in just in time. The … the Reapers know who I am. Anyone who worked for Rees is a target. You're the only person I can trust, because you were the only person your father would trust and that's good enough for me.'

I can feel Sophy's hand in mine and I close my fist around it. 'What do I have to do?'

He steps back into the room and uncovers a tall steel drum.

'OK,' I say, 'and … how?'

He shakes his head and Keeling says to him, 'We need to get you out of here. They're coming. You've got about two minutes.'

'Eh?' I say.

'There's transport, a helicopter waiting to take Dr Yeo and Dr Conway. It's not safe for them to stay. Once they've gone, as long as you can do this, we'll make an announcement – disperse these crowds.'

'Good,' says Conway, 'we're going into hiding. Scotland – a secure military base in the highlands – if we make it.' He's looking at Keeling as he speaks. 'We're going to work on this full time from there.'

'What about us?' I say.

'Well, you'll be safe. You're immune.'

'And her?' I say.

He turns to look at Sophy, raises an eyebrow. 'Well, if you needed another incentive to do this quickly, there it is.'

'You bastard.' I feel that blackness sweeping over me like a load of angry crows. Keeling gets in between us but Conway goes on: 'Ben, you can do this. You take the drum to the dispersal cage. Two metres below us, there's a network of tunnels. One of them leads to an underground chamber specially designed for this exact job.'

I push Keeling aside. 'Vaccinate her. Now.'

'We have to leave. I can't –'

'Fucking NOW! Do it! Or I'm not doing anything.'

'Ben, it's OK,' says Sophy, her hand on my arm. But Dr Yeo is unlocking a secure steel box and pulling out a slim glass tube with a stopper, one of many.

He unwraps a plastic hypodermic. 'Ben, it's not perfect,' he says. 'It's –'

'Just do it.'

She looks at me as he drives it into her arm. 'Josh,' she says, 'he wasn't … it wasn't anything, just … he was kind to me.'

I nod. 'It's OK, I know that, I just wish I'd been here, that's all.' I ask Keeling, 'Where do we go?'

A clattering and shouting from outside in the corridor. I can hear doors being opened and slammed, the stamping of boots. A gun shot.

'Shit!' says Keeling. He pulls out his radio.

Conway steps up. He's calm, icy. He pushes his glasses back on his head. 'Go through here,' he points to the door at the other end of the lab. 'That'll take you onto a further corridor. You're going right, you're always going right – remember that if you get lost. There's only one door on that corridor. You open it and it looks like a cleaners' cupboard: mops and detergents and so on, but at the back, behind a shelving unit, is a narrow door. The code pad is set into the wall. You'll need this to see it.'

He hands me a tiny steel torch. 'The code pad is in fluorescent ink, this is an ultraviolet torch. Shine this on it and it'll appear on the wall. The code is 92778HR, OK?'

I nod, repeat it. 'And then?' I hear Sophy shiver next to me.

'You'll see. Keep going right and just let it go. Every drop,' is all he says.

More gun shots. Conway turns for a moment in the direction of the noise then back to me. 'You need to go. Good luck.' Breathless now, he grabs a face mask and throws one to Yeo. 'Quick! Put this on. I need to collect some samples from the tanks.'

'Hurry up!' says Keeling.

Sophy and I tip the steel drum back and wheel it from the room. We're backing out and I'm pulling it and I can see Conway in the eerie gloom of the tank chamber dipping in and out of view, leaning over his fleshy charges until the door snaps shut behind us.

32

We're alone in the corridor. It's quiet for maybe 30 seconds but they're coming. Boots, fists, and thick voices raised. The stairways will be filling with them now.

'Here!' Sophy says, 'in here!'

The door opens onto a small cupboard as he described. There's a massive floor cleaner like a lawnmower, stuck in the middle of it, and we pull it out into the corridor to make space. I check for the torch in my pocket and then together we pull the drum into the tiny room. In front of us is the shelving unit. My bad arm is aching but I make it work, and where the cast is cracked, I break it back so I can use my hand. I tug at the unit but it doesn't budge. All I do is dislodge a canister of floor polish which hits the floor and breaks. A tar-like ooze starts seeping from the crack.

'It's bolted. It's bolted to the fucking wall!'

We look around the room. There are brooms, mops, buckets and industrial size detergent cans. No bolt cutters or screwdrivers. Not even a hammer.

'Maybe it's caught?' says Sophy.

'Caught? On what? I'm telling you it's screwed to the wall.'

'Shush!" she puts her hand to her mouth. Voices outside. 'Shit,' I breathe.

'Look!' she points to the door. A long steel bolt is drawn at the very top. I just get there. Just in time. Just as someone on the other side starts to kick at the door, I reach up and slide the bolt home. I can hear someone – a Scottish accent: 'Someone's in there! Listen! Shut it – listen!' They're quiet. And we're quiet.

It won't hold forever.

They start up their kicking and I can see the bolt bend and bow with every blow.

'We'll just have to rip it off the wall,' I say. 'Just get back, far as you can against the door.'

I take the sides of the unit in each hand and I wrench at it. Bottles and cans slide from side to side and another can clatters to the floor. I'm pulling back with all my strength when I hear Sophy.

'Lift it,' she's saying.

'I am lifting it, what's it look like I'm doing?' I snap back.

'No,' she's next to me now, 'You're pulling it. Just lift it, you know, unhook it. I think it's just sitting on the bolts. I think you can …'

And I see she's right. She joins me and we push it up and back against the wall and it lifts away towards us. We stack it on the empty wall and I'm just feeling for the torch when the bolt blows behind us and the door is pushed open. Two men, thick set, both wearing balaclavas shoulder their way into the room. 'What's going on?' says the Scottish accent.

'Who the fuck are you?' says his friend. And then I see his eyes in their woollen slits dart and rest on the steel drum. He moves towards it. 'Is this what I think it is?' he says.

'Grab her,' says the Scot and the other pulls at Sophy and starts to drag her out into the corridor shouting as he goes. I go after him and the other one stops me at the door.

I slow my breathing. This is easy. I bring my elbow up and smack him square up through his face. Blood pushes up onto exposed skin. I aim a push kick and hear his ribs crack against the sole of my boot. The other guy has his arm around Sophy's neck and is dragging her back, shouting behind him for back up. When he sees his mate, he stops and pulls her head back. 'Woah,' he says. 'You watch yourself, you're not going anywhere. Just back the fuck up. BACK UP!' he shouts. 'Back up and bring that thing out here.'

I stare at him. I know the others are coming. A tiny pearl of sweat hovers on his eyelash and he blinks it free. Sophy looks at me and I nod. She shifts her weight and hangs her head low for a moment then brings it back up sharp against his skull. He's knocked back by it but he comes back at her and, before I can stop him, punches her hard in her side. She goes down, winded and I come for him then. And suddenly he's all the people that ever hurt her or me. I lock my fingers and pull his head towards me and knee him once, twice, in the chest and lay him out with a knee to the head. And I don't even think about it.

Sophy's on her feet but she's hurt. I grab her hand and pull her into the cupboard and haul the shelving unit against the door.

Footsteps and voices. The others are here.

'Sophy, push it. Push against the shelves as hard as you can!' I cry, and she leans into it, weathering the pounding from the other side.

I hold up the torch and punch in the code in the purple light.

More banging on the door.

And then we're moving. A thin steel mesh slides down around us and the floor starts to sink and the room isn't a room or a cupboard anymore, it's a lift. We leave the walls and the shelves and the door behind, and the cage drives us further underground. We're travelling at speed, whistling past walls of black brick and all around the air is wet and dank. There's a rushing sound coming up from below.

And just as suddenly it stops with a shudder and I find the catch and the mesh slides back. Ahead of us a tunnel curves away into darkness. I look back at Sophy; her face is a greenish white. 'Are you OK?'

'I think he broke a rib,' she smiles.

'You were brilliant, head-butting him like that.'

'Er … yeah. Ben, how did you know … I mean, you were like – like Batman or something. I didn't know you –'

'I did some fighting in China. I'm not proud of it. I wouldn't … I mean –'

'It's just … you weren't yourself. It was scary.'

'I know. I wasn't. I'm not. I don't even know if I can be again.'

She holds my hand and her palm is wet and warm. 'You will be,' she says.

I shrug. 'Maybe. With you, maybe.'

I drag the steel drum out on its castors and turn to Sophy. 'You want to wait here?'

But she's already shaking her head. 'Really?'

Backs bent, we trundle the drum along the tunnel. As it bends away from the lift shaft we go in total darkness. There's the sound of our breathing and the wheels of the drum and faint, far away, the rushing, gurgling noise I heard before.

We come to a place where the tunnel forks and we stop. Sophy's breathing hard and clutching her side. 'You want to stop for a bit?' I ask, but again she says no.

'Which way?'

'Right, he said, always keep going right. That must be it.'

On we go, water in runnels under our feet, bent double under the tunnel roof and the rushing noise getting closer. The air is fuller now, richer. It smells of earth and sky and iron.

We round another bend, feeling our way in the blackness, our hands on wet brick, and there, in the distance, a tiny pinprick of orange light.

As we get closer, I can see Sophy's face and the broad gleam of the steel on the belly of the drum. The noise is deafening now. A low roaring that starts from below and echoes up and around the walls. It spins around us and carries us forward into the light.

A low arch. Light streaming.

We dip down, pulling and pushing the drum through, and emerge into a huge circular chamber with a vaulted roof. We're on a galleried walkway that runs all around the edge. Arc lights blaze high above us in what looks like a canopy of tubes and hydraulics.

Far below us a vast, depthless basin of water churns and boils. A narrow walkway like a kind of wire rope-bridge pushes out from the edge where we stand, suspended from above over the water. I turn to Sophy. We're both wet from the spray and shivering.

I have to shout to be heard. 'This is it. It must be. Every drop, he said.' She looks at me and nods.

We wheel the drum around to the where the bridge starts. It leads out to a tiny circular platform at the end.

I pull the drum onto the walkway, and the weight of it makes it sway from side to side. I grip the rail with wet hands and breathe. Sophy steps on but I say, 'I'll do it. There's no point both of us. Too heavy,' I add, when

I see the look in her eyes. She steps back.

I go on my hands and knees, ignoring the pain in my broken arm, nudging the drum forward high above the seething water, I can taste the ozone on my tongue. I rattle forward on the swinging bridge till I reach the platform. I get to my feet and turn back to see Sophy, her hands in her hair, her face fixed.

I unpin the lid of the drum, it's full to the brim of a violet coloured liquid. Very slowly I tip the canister and drain the liquid into the water below. I crane my neck to see the water glow a fluorescent purple, leaving a thin web like plankton on the surface and then it's gone.

I walk back along the bridge over the water to where Sophy's waiting for me. And there, under the vaulted roof that fizzes with light, high above the frothing water, I push her back against the brick and I kiss her hard on the mouth.

33

We walked out of Rees. Just walked out like nothing had happened. Picked our way through blood and clubs and broken glass. People were leaving, wandering, dazed. One woman with bright eyes over her mask told me we were saved, that someone had said the vaccine would be in the water, and that all anyone had to do was drink it. She took off her mask and hugged me.

I thought about the creatures in the tanks below us and I felt sick.

When we got back to Sophy's we found Maurice there, smelling of soap, with his leg in clean bandages, and Sophy's Mum talking to Charlie. Maurice looked up when I came in and he gave me this weird shrug and a smile and it nearly finished me. He's going to be OK though. Sometimes I look at him and I see Lee sitting in my cell, his face wreathed in smiles and his belly gurgling.

He's going to live with me for the time being.
Jo comes to see him most days. He's talking about
restocking the shop, starting up again. I said I'd help
him out, and he looked genuinely pleased. The other
day I was going out and they were sitting there together
eating biscuits, and before I left him, he leaned forward,
spraying biscuit crumbs onto the floor and grabbed my
hand. 'You're a lovely young man, Benny. Rinky Dinky.
Eh Jo?' she nodded and under their gaze, under my skin,
I could feel myself cooking.

The vaccination programme's working well. All
major towns and cities here and in the US are well
stocked, and apart from the odd isolated case, it's well
and truly dealt with. It seems either Rees or Dad was
wrong about the hit rate of the virus. It seems there
were a good many people who had a natural immunity
to it. When they tested her, they found Sophy was one
of them.

I had a message from China last week, from a small
town in a far northern province. From Rooster: he'd
found me through Facebook. All it said was, 'We are
safe. All safe. Good luck.'

The Reapers disbanded. Some of them were found
and put on trial. Two of our neighbours were in with
them, people we'd known forever.

When Sophy and I came back from Rees, it was
getting dark. A storm was starting up. We sat in the car
at the top of her road and she leant against my arm,
and her head and her hair was on my shoulder, and I

don't know I've wanted anything more than I wanted her that night.

And later, much later, after all the talking and all the tears, she locked her arm in mine and we went slowly up the stairs to her room, to her bed and we lay together and held each other without speaking until dawn came and I slept.

THE END

ACKNOWLEDGMENTS

As ever, I must thank my family and my friends for their unfailing help and support as I wrote this:

Mike, thank you for the design. I love-not-hate it.

Roo, plot wizard.

Stew … just wow!

TB. I love you.

JB, JB, and OB. You are top of the league.

Lisa, thank you for your brilliant editing
(and everything, everything else!)

Thanks also, to the London Shootfighters gym
(www.londonshootfighters.com) for letting a batty
middle-aged author come and watch the incredibly
talented MMA fighters training, and ask lots
of silly questions.

If you enjoyed it, please do leave a review on Amazon.

It makes a HUGE difference to small publishers.